HOT
PROPERTY

SUSANNE
O'LEARY

HOT PROPERTY
By Susanne O'Leary

Cover design and typesetting by JD Smith Design

CHAPTER 1

"'To my great-niece, Megan O'Farrell, daughter of my nephew, Sean, I bequeath my house at Kilshee, County Kerry and all the land thereof.'"

Megan blinked and stared at the young solicitor, momentarily forgetting the cold air creeping up her bare legs in the small office. Having nearly drifted off while he droned on about inheritance laws and other legal gobbledygook, she was now wide awake.

"House? Old Uncle Pat willed me his house? That lovely little farmhouse?" She paused, trying to take it in. "And the land thereof? So there's land as well as a house?"

"Yes. Ten acres." He smiled. "Congratulations. I'm sure it was a pleasant surprise."

"Yes, of course." Megan was stunned. This was like a dream. She instantly imagined herself in that cute little house by the sea, with a turf fire burning in the grate and the smell of roast lamb wafting around. "I didn't know exactly what I'd inherited. I was hoping it would be some money. I could do with a bit of cash right now."

His eyes twinkled. "Couldn't we all? But this is even better, isn't it?"

"You bet." Megan beamed at him. "A house," she mumbled, "a little house by the sea…"

"Excellent location," the solicitor said. "A spit from the

ocean, at the foot of the Benoskee mountain. Wonderful views and great walking, if you're into hillwalking." He glanced at her shoes. "But perhaps not."

She looked down at her strappy sandals. "Well," she started, "I would naturally *change* my shoes if I were to go hillwalking." She tugged at her skirt, regretting her choice of clothing, but it had been hot and sunny in Dublin when she left early that morning. There, in the south west, it was misty and chilly.

"Of course. But you don't look like the outdoorsy type."

Annoyed by the slight scorn in his voice, Megan shook back her hair. "You mean because I don't have chunky, hairy legs and a butch hairdo? Actually, if that's what it takes—" she glanced at the little sign on his desk, "Mr Nolan, I wouldn't be interested in climbing hills."

"Right," he muttered, his voice cooler. He turned back to the document. "So, there we are. You're the proud owner of a house."

"In the Kingdom," Megan added.

He glanced at her. "Are you taking the mickey?"

"Taking the—what?"

"Taking the mickey," he repeated. "As in being ironic."

"Why? Isn't that what they call Kerry? The Kingdom?"

"Yes. But it depends on the way you say it. It can sound like a sneer."

"Why would I sneer at Kerry?"

He shrugged. "Oh, I don't know. Dublin socialite, slumming it, popped into my mind. Having a laugh at the peasants."

Megan bristled. "You're very quick to judge by appearances, I see."

"Well, a person's appearance is often a good hint of their general lifestyle and attitudes, I find. As a lawyer, I often have to make a quick assessment."

"And how often do you get it wrong?"

He grinned. "Never."

She smirked. "You just did."

His smile stiffened. "That's a first." He adopted a more serious expression. "Are you married? Sorry, but I have to ask. For the purposes of the registration of the property."

"Can't you tell? I mean your powers of observation being so great, one would expect you to know whether I'm a married or a single 'socialite'." Megan drew breath. She knew she sounded bitchy but the way he was sizing her up made her feel uncomfortable.

"I take it you're not," he retorted.

"What makes you say that?"

"No wedding ring. And…uh, your general attitude."

"What's wrong with it?"

"Oh, I don't know. You seem a little prickly."

Megan straightened up on the rickety chair. "I must say *your* attitude is, uh, a little unprofessional, if you don't mind my saying so." She was going to add that his white fisherman's sweater and jeans were not appropriate for a solicitor but changed her mind. Why sink to his level?

Their eyes locked for a loaded minute or so, until Nolan turned back to his document. "You're right. Please accept my sincere apologies."

Megan sighed, too tired to keep up the fight. "Apology accepted. Sorry if I seem a little irritable but I'm very tired. I got up at dawn to drive down here from Dublin, and I haven't had any breakfast. So, maybe we could get back to business? I'm sure you have other clients who need your attention. Or you have to go and defend someone in court or something."

"Yes, I do actually." He cleared his throat. "So, married or single?"

Is being newly divorced 'single', she wondered. She found it hard to say the word 'divorced'. It was an admittance of failure, somehow, of not having succeeded in keeping a man.

Of having been rejected. Even saying that word brought her back to a place she was trying to forget. "I'm not married," she said after a moment's deliberation.

He wrote something on the document, then glanced up. "In a relationship?"

She let out a little laugh. "Sounds like something from Facebook."

He coloured slightly. "I do have to ask these questions, you know."

"I see. Okay. No, I'm not in a relationship. At the moment."

"Right." He scribbled something. Then he looked up. "You're on Facebook?"

"Isn't everyone?"

"I suppose." He peered at her. "You have a lot of friends there?"

"Uh, yes. Twelve," Megan said without thinking. "—hundred," she added, to make it sound less pathetic.

He looked at her with respect. "You have twelve hundred friends on Facebook?"

She met his gaze. "That's right."

"Amazing. I only have two hundred or something. But I don't spend much time on it."

Tired, fed up and now so hungry, the rumble of her stomach echoed around the small room, Megan sighed. "Neither do I. Can we sort this out, and then I'll sign on the dotted line. Once I have the keys, I can go and take a look at the house."

"I'm afraid that won't be possible."

Megan stared at him. "What? You've just told me I owned a house and then—"

Nolan sighed. "I explained all that before I read the will. It's the subject of probate."

"Probate? Uh, what does that actually mean?"

Nolan adopted a business-like expression. "Probate is a way to determine who has ownership of the property and allows those who may have unpaid debts or bills to make a claim against the estate. There's a probate court which works with this type of thing. It involves executing the will or establishing a means of disposing of property when there isn't a will."

Megan blinked. "Oh, I see. But there *is* a will."

He nodded. "Yes, but it has to be established that your uncle was actually the only owner of the property when he died."

"But isn't that the job of the executor?"

"Yes," Nolan said. "And I'm the executor. Unusual, but your uncle appointed me because he said he trusted me. He didn't really explain why he wanted you to have the house, though. Do you know?"

"No. Other than that it should have gone to my dad, but he died two years ago. I didn't even know Uncle Pat that well. We spent a summer with him when I was eight but I haven't seen him since. My dad didn't talk about him much or had any contact with him, as far as I know."

He studied her for a moment. "You're very like your uncle, you know."

"Am I? I don't remember what he looked like."

"Red hair, brown eyes. Just like you. The same strong chin." He nodded. "Yes. You're the image of him."

"I look like my dad, everyone says. But maybe Uncle Pat and he were alike, then."

"Probably. And your uncle had no children of his own…" Nolan shuffled through his papers. "I think it said something about not wanting to give it to those who didn't deserve it. I had it here somewhere."

Megan tried to curb her impatience. She wanted to get out of there, have something to eat and then drive around for a bit to get her bearings. Daniel Nolan was a good-looking man, with his hazel eyes, thick, sandy hair and tall frame, but there was something about him that made her bristle.

"Never mind," she said. "I'm sure there was a good reason. How long will the probate court take?"

Nolan shrugged. "Depends. Could take a couple of months or a year."

"Oh shit," Megan blurted out.

"Quite." Then he seemed unable to hold in the smile she suspected had been hovering on his lips for some time. His white teeth against his light tan instantly took years off him. "I know. It would piss me off big time, too."

Megan couldn't help returning his smile. "Well, I suppose I'll just have to be patient."

"What do you think you'll do with it?"

"What?"

"I mean, are you keeping it or are you going to sell it?"

"I don't really know," Megan said. "I'd like to see it first."

"If you want to sell, let me know. It's in a very good location and would sell quickly. The land could be sold separately as grazing land. Farmers in the area are always looking for extra fields."

"Okay. I'll think about it."

"It's pretty wrecked, you know. It'll take a lot of work to make it habitable."

Megan stood up. "We'll see. I might be able to do it up myself. I'm pretty good with a hammer and nails."

"It's more than banging a few nails into a wall, I'm afraid. Or hanging up pretty curtains. It'll be a while before you can invite your trendy friends over from Dublin."

"I might find a builder willing to give me a good price," Megan said, trying to look as if restoring houses was something she did as a hobby.

He laughed. "Around here? This is Kerry, not Dublin. Builders are scarce, and a cheap, honest one even scarcer."

Megan sighed. "I suppose. I'll wait and see. Right now, I just want to go and have some breakfast and then get going. It's a long drive back."

He rose. "You know, you could go and have a look at the house if you want. I can't give you the keys, but no harm done if you just have a look from the outside."

She was going to say no and flaunt out of his office, but her curiosity got the better of her. "That would be great."

"I could come with you, if you can wait until lunchtime."

"No thank you. I can manage all by myself. Just tell me where it is, and I'll be on my way."

He picked up a brochure. "Here's a very good map and a description of the house. It was done before your uncle died. He was thinking of selling, as he was in a nursing home then. But he died before he had a chance to go through with it. We got a few very good offers, actually."

"We?"

He nodded. "Yes, my dad is an estate agent, and we often work together. Those offers are still on the table. We told the prospective buyers we would ask you what you wanted to do and let them know."

Megan stood at the door, hesitating. "How much did they offer?"

"With the land, two hundred and fifty K. Just the house and the small garden, a hundred and fifty K."

"K? You mean thousand? Two hundred and fifty thousand? Euros?"

He smirked. "No, peanuts."

"Ha, ha." Megan took the brochure and stuffed it into her tote bag. "I'll decide when the time comes." She held out her hand. "Goodbye, and thanks for your help."

He took Megan's hand and held it a moment longer than absolutely necessary. "You're welcome. By the way, there's a restaurant down the street, where you can get breakfast. I get the feeling you need 'the full Irish.'"

Megan wrinkled her nose. "Never touch that horrible stuff."

He laughed. "No, I suppose it's not very healthy. But

sometimes it's a great pick-me-up after a heavy night. They do a good one there few people can say no to."

"I'm sure I can resist the temptation."

He grinned. "You're probably not that easy to seduce."

"Not with sausage and bacon in any case." Megan withdrew her hand. "Goodbye, Mr Nolan."

"Goodbye." He winked. "Enjoy the breakfast."

* * *

Half an hour later, Megan looked at a plate with two fried eggs, several strips of fatty bacon, two pork sausages, a grilled tomato, three slices of black pudding and a pile of fried mushrooms. She had intended to order a cup of tea and a brown scone, but to her annoyance, Daniel Nolan was right. The smell that permeated the small restaurant was too much for her tired brain to resist. "This is it?" she said to the waitress. "The full Irish?"

She nodded. "That's it. Are you sure you have enough there?"

Megan looked at the plate. "Enough to feed a family of five, you mean? Yes, I think that should keep them happy for about a week."

The waitress giggled and left, with Megan wondering how she could possibly eat even half of it. But the smell was so delicious she decided to have a nibble, although it must have added up to her normal calorie intake for a whole week. The nibble turned into several bites. Before she could stop herself, she had eaten the whole lot, along with two slices of brown soda bread and some toast and marmalade.

Feeling guilty, she glanced through the window to make sure Nolan wasn't walking past on his way to court. She didn't want to give him the satisfaction of knowing he had been right. She told herself that she wouldn't eat anything for the rest of the day. An easy promise to keep, as she had never in her life been so full. But it all seemed to have loaded her brain with feel-good hormones, and she stepped into the wind and rain outside, feeling bright and cheerful.

The drive to the house took about half an hour from Tralee. Megan passed through Camp taking the right turn on the road toward Castlegregory, along the Atlantic coast. The sun appeared from behind the clouds, turning the water of Tralee Bay deep turquoise. With the dramatic backdrop of majestic mountains, it was the most stunning scenery she had ever seen. She had trouble keeping her eyes on the road, wanting to take in all the beautiful sights. The blue sky. The endless ocean. Seagulls gliding, dipping, rising again. She had to stop several times to allow her senses to absorb it all.

On an impulse, she drove past the turning she should have taken, continuing on, past the village out towards Brandon, turning up the road to the Connor pass. She wanted to get up there to see the views of the whole of Dingle, so she could get an idea of the landscape and the setting of this peninsula she hadn't visited for so many years. After driving up the scary hairpin bends, she finally reached the top of the pass and the viewing point.

She got out of the car, looked to the north side of the peninsula and recognised Castlegregory, that lovely decrepit old village with its tangle of cottages and Victorian houses. Further out, the Maharees, with its low-lying landscape, a scimitar of sand edged with long golden beaches, pushed flat and green into the wind-ruffled water of Tralee Bay. The mountains of the Dingle Peninsula, the long spine of Slieve Mish inland, the hills around Mount Brandon away in the west across Brandon Bay, outlined in dove grey and pink against the ever-changing sky. And the Atlantic spread out below, the intense blue meeting the sky at the horizon and the waves crashing onto the rocks.

She hadn't been here since she was eight, and she kept

asking herself why the family never returned after that summer. She vaguely remembered some kind of argument that went on late into the night toward the end of the holiday. Angry voices woke her up. Frightened by shouting, she lay in her bed, wondering what it was all about. The next day, stiff goodbyes, and her father's silence during the drive home confused her. No mention of Uncle Pat since then. What happened? What was that row about? So many unanswered questions she had never bothered to ask. She chided herself for not taking the trouble.

She stood there, mesmerised by all the beautiful sights, for a long time before she got into the car and drove down the twists and turns again, until she was back on the main road, a little disoriented and dizzy. Where was she going now?

Megan pulled in at the roadside to consult the map, comparing it to the description in the brochure. There was a photo of a small, white house on the front page. It looked to be in quite good nick: the typical Kerry farmhouse, with roses climbing over the front door. A sweet little garden with daisies, blue hydrangeas and what looked like an apple tree at the gate. There was a ruin beside the stream, she remembered. The remnants of a fifteenth-century fortified farm, which added a romantic feel to the place. The picture-perfect weekend retreat. –*This could become my haven, my bolt hole, where I will go to escape the sorrow of the break up...* She flinched at the memory of Stephen's betrayal and the pain it had brought.

Turning off the main road, she drove into a small lane full of potholes. The car wobbled up the road, past a farm, a shed and then... a house.

Megan brought the car to a screeching halt. Her heart sinking, she stared at the house. Was this it? This crumbling wreck with broken windows, peeling paint, sagging roof and overgrown garden? It was surrounded by ragged fields on either side, where sheep and cattle grazed.

Megan pulled up beside the broken fence. She looked from the brochure to the house. Yes. There was no mistake. The 'dream house' she had inherited was a wreck. Stunned, Megan sat there for a while. The photo must have been taken a long time ago, when the house was occupied. Now, it didn't look as if anyone had lived in it for years.

Sell it, was her first thought. Sell it quick and get rid of it. "Two hundred and fifty thousand," Daniel Nolan said, "including the fields." It seemed the best option. The only option. A rather wonderful option. Images of holidays in the Bahamas, shopping trips to New York and the possibility of buying an apartment in Dublin popped into her mind.

After the divorce and the sale of the house she owned with her husband, she couldn't afford to buy anything decent and ended up in a tiny rented flat. This house looked like a ticket to a better existence. The idyll of being hostess to some snooty Dublin freeloaders slowly faded, replaced by the buzz of financial independence. A quarter of a million. Not to be sneezed at.

Megan got out of the car and looked around. The setting was certainly stunning. Mountains rising up just behind the back fields. Breathtaking views of dunes and the deep blue ocean from the front gate. A ruined tower with mellow grey stones and crumbling turrets around which swallows swooped in a graceful ballet. Someone with a lot of money could turn this into the gem it once was. Someone who would see the potential, imagine sitting on the front step with a cup of tea, looking at the sea. Or having breakfast on the cement slab at the back, which could be made into a patio, where the sun would turn the top of the mountain pink in the early morning. *Stop it*, she told herself. *This isn't a dream you could possibly realise.*

Megan walked to the front door and peered in through the little window at the top. Seeing nothing but a dusty stone flagged floor, she decided to go around the house to the back.

Hearing a gurgling sound as she wobbled around the outside of the house on her high heels, she discovered a stream at the bottom of the garden, where water rushed over boulders and rocks. She jumped at a flapping behind a tree. A heron rose and glided along the water, disappearing around the bend further up.

Megan turned to study the back of the house. It seemed even worse from this side. The back door was hanging off its hinges, and most of the panes in the windows were broken. But the sun had come out of the clouds and shone on the little patio. With the sound of the stream and a lone thrush singing nearby, the peace was nearly spiritual.

She plucked up enough courage to go to the back door, telling herself she had to get inside. She remembered Daniel Nolan's warning. She wasn't the rightful owner yet. Going inside would be trespassing. But wasn't even walking into the garden trespassing? If the deed was already done, what harm would one step further do? She pushed at the door. It creaked open.

The dark interior, dimly illuminated by a sunbeam where dust particles danced like smoke from a dying fire, felt gloomy and brooding. Megan let her hand fall and stepped back. *I'd better not. I'll get in the car and go home.* But as if something inside was beckoning, she felt compelled to push at the door again and step inside.

CHAPTER 2

Megan stood in the lean-to kitchen. This was a new addition. In the old days, the big room to the right of the front door was the kitchen-cum-living room. She remembered it had a big solid fuel stove and an inglenook fireplace, where a turf fire burned every single day of the year. The house was two hundred years old and hadn't changed or been added to much during that time. The family lived, cooked and took their meals in that big room, as it was always warm.

To the left was the parlour, not used much, except at times of family gatherings, Christmas, Easter, wakes, christenings and weddings. This room had been furnished with a chintzy sofa and two easy chairs, a wobbly coffee table. A big glassed-in cupboard full of silver, Waterford crystal and framed photos of long-dead relatives. A framed photo of President Kennedy and his wife on one wall and a picture of the Sacred Heart of Christ on the other. She remembered staring up at the two pictures, admiring Jackie Kennedy's beautiful face and being a little frightened of the bleeding heart in the open chest of Jesus. They didn't spend much time in that room. Upstairs, there were two big bedrooms and a small box room, turned into a bathroom.

Megan wrinkled her nose at the smell of damp and rat's urine and continued down the corridor into the big room, once the original kitchen-cum-living room.

She instantly recognised the fireplace with padded seats on either side. And the wheel by the wall that was a kind of bellows to keep the fire going, that Uncle Pat operated with great skill, the flames falling and rising at his command. At eight, she was fascinated by it and asked to turn the wheel. Uncle Pat took her hand and made her turn the handle faster and faster, then slowing down, then turning it again when the fire threatened to die.

The seats were still there, the fabric faded and full of holes. She sat down on one of them. Breathing in the stale smell of old smoke, she was back at that magic time when everything was an adventure.

Long-forgotten memories slowly returned. The kind faces of Uncle Pat and Auntie Molly. The silky fur of the kitten they gave her. Going out in the early morning to the little barn to milk the two cows. The smell of warm milk and sunshine. Collecting eggs from the hen house. The clucking of the hens as they picked at the ground. Digging for new potatoes, then eating them hot, with butter and salt. Making scones with Aunt Molly, mixing the dough in the yellow bowl at the kitchen table that was, miraculously, still there by the window.

Megan got up and opened the shutters. Light cascaded into the room, revealing shabby remnants of better days. Wallpaper hung off the walls, and plaster from the ceiling crumbled onto dirty floorboards. But the room still held all the memories so close to her heart. Despite the smell of mould and smoke, a warm blanket of comfort settled on her shoulders. A feeling of coming home, of being welcome. She sighed, soothed by the soft light and peace in the little house.

A shrill sound pierced the silence. Irritated, Megan looked around. Her phone ringing in her bag had broken the spell. She fished it out. The number was unfamiliar.

"Hello?" she snapped.

"Hi there. Dan Nolan here. You're at the house?"

"Yes. So?"

"Well, I just thought I'd tell you there's good news. Two pieces of good news, actually."

"What are they?" Megan demanded.

"First, I've just talked to someone at the probate court, who said he thought this would go through very quickly. So you could be all sorted in a month or two. And the second piece of good news is that the offer from one of the buyers is still good. "Two hundred and fifty K for the lot, they said, once the probate thing has been finalised."

Megan's heart skipped a beat. "Two hundred and... I mean... oh...God, I don't know what to say."

"Just say yes," Daniel Nolan suggested. "Then you can go out and celebrate."

"I suppose." Megan hesitated. Her legs weak, she sat down on the little seat by the fireplace again. "But, Mr Nolan—"

"Dan," he corrected, "as we'll probably see a lot of each other in the near future."

"Okay," she said automatically, her mind whirling.

"Are you at the house right now?"

"Yes."

He laughed. "I suppose you can see what a wreck it is, then."

"Yes."

"And that restoring it would cost an arm and a leg, a lot of trouble and hard work?"

Megan looked at the view of the ocean and the white sails far out in the bay. "Yes."

"An impossible task, right?"

"Yes."

The phone still to her ear, Megan walked down the corridor and out of the house. She sank down on the back step, where the warm sunshine felt good after the chilly gloom inside. She squealed as something small and feathery scurried over her foot.

"What was that?" Dan asked at the other end.

"Oh, just a mouse running over my foot." She looked closer at the small creature on the concrete. "No, not a mouse," she corrected herself, "a lizard. Oh, it's so cute."

"Yes. Okay. Right." He paused. "I'll be in touch once I have some news."

* * *

The trip back was endless. Not only because she was tired, but also because tearing herself away from the little house, the views and the sheer magic of the place had been such a wrench. Did everyone feel like her when they were at that particular place? Or was it her memories that sparked off these vibes?

She knew she should jump at the chance of selling the wrecked house for enough money to change her life for the better. She could quit her job, take a sabbatical or do a course in something like computer graphics and then get a better job. Maybe even set up a business. Buy a little apartment, as property prices had lowered. Take a trip to somewhere exotic. Put away a little cash for a rainy day. Have more security. It all made a lot of sense—more sense than hanging on to a wreck that would only end up costing a fortune to restore, even if all she bought was a bed and a couple of chairs in IKEA.

The house needed a lot of work, even if the roof seemed quite sound to her untrained eyes. The kitchen and bathroom needed updating. The house needed to be rewired and the walls insulated. So much work and no money. Madness. *Sell*, she told herself, *it's the only option.*

* * *

"Cutbacks," the manager said. "We're not going to supply this service anymore."

Megan took a deep breath, trying to appear cool. "You mean, you're not going to offer your customers the advice of a personal shopper? Or a stylist? But how about the other branches? The one on the south side—"

He sighed theatrically. "No. Afraid not. There are no positions available anywhere. Of course, we'll give you severance pay. Two months' salary in lieu of notice."

There was a brief silence, during which Megan knew she was supposed to say 'thank you' and 'I understand. Not your fault.' But she got up from the chair without a word and left, slamming the door. She didn't need to be polite to him anymore. There was no need to suck up to the arrogant bastard, she thought with a feeling of relief.

Back in her own cubby hole of an office, she immediately packed the few little bits that decorated her desk. A blue Bausch & Lomb coffee mug, a cactus in a pot, all her coloured pencils. Even the little brass plaque that said: 'Megan O'Farrell, stylist.'

She took the framed diploma from her haute-couture course in Paris off the wall, followed by the photo of her with the head of Dior and the one of a well-known actress with a signed dedication. Her hands shook as she put them in a cardboard box. She thought of those happy days when she had studied fashion in Paris and had worked so hard for her diploma and been ecstatic when she got her first job with a London fashion photographer, styling his models and organising photo shoots. Then going back to her Dublin roots and getting this job, first as assistant buyer and then stylist and personal shopper. Meeting Stephen and their whirlwind romance. The glamorous wedding and romantic honeymoon in Bermuda. Oh God, those were the days…

Then it hit her. She had lost her job. Her knees shaking, she flopped onto the chair, gripped the armrests and steeled herself not to cry, but failed. She let the tears run unchecked as the disappointment and anger welled up in her chest.

After sobbing for a few minutes, she wiped her eyes, blew her nose and got up again. *Shut up and stop moaning*, she told herself.

She gathered her things and left the office, collecting her last pay cheque from the secretary in accounts, who whispered she was sorry. "Nothing much we can do about it. They're cutting down on staff everywhere. It's terrible."

"Yes," Megan sighed. "I must think about getting another job now."

"I'm sure it won't take you long." The girl picked up a magazine. "I read your horoscope just now. Do you want to hear it?"

Megan shrugged. "I don't really believe in all that stuff but go ahead."

"Okay. Here it is: *Your newest project needs more attention than you may have thought at first, so make sure you're giving it your all. That almost certainly means that you must leave old problems behind and look forward to a new beginning. Being gentle and kind-hearted, romantic and sensitive, you must try not to be influenced by the wrong people...*" The receptionist drew breath. "See? Your future looks good."

Megan laughed. "I wish. And the bit about being kind-hearted isn't exactly correct today. I have really bad thoughts about that bastard."

"But you *are* very kind-hearted," the girl argued. "You've been so nice to me always. You changed my life when you taught me how to dress."

"I wouldn't go that far."

"But you did," the girl insisted. "You were like a fairy godmother. Peter wouldn't have given me a second glance, if it hadn't been for your makeover. But look at us now." She waggled her third finger, where a diamond ring gleamed. "Engaged. All because of you."

Megan smiled at the memory. "It was fun. And you had great potential. You just needed a little nudge."

The girl sighed and looked at Megan with admiration. "You're better than any psychologist. You pulled me out of the dumps in an afternoon. A heart of gold, that's what you have. Like all Cancers."

"Don't forget the negative attributes," Megan remarked. "I'm moody and over-sensitive. Good at bearing a grudge and always looking for revenge."

The receptionist put down her magazine. "Who doesn't? I'd love to strangle all the people in management."

Megan put the cheque in her bag. "Don't we all? Bye for now. Good luck in finding another job."

"Thanks. The same to you. And don't forget to be careful about the wrong people. And give that new project your all."

Megan winked. "I will. When I find it."

* * *

She spotted him before he saw her: Stephen, her ex-husband, out shopping with his new wife. Megan hesitated between slinking away and going up to them to say hello. Before she could decide, he had seen her. Megan felt her face redden and took a step back, nearly knocking over a display of scarves and handbags.

"Megan."

"Stephen," she chortled. "What a surprise. And—" she glanced at the woman trying to shrink behind him, "Laura, isn't it?"

"Yes." Stephen put a protective arm around her. "I was going to call you."

Megan lifted an eyebrow. "About?"

"The house. The one in Kerry. Your mother told me about

it."

Megan bristled. "My mother? You spoke to my mother?"

"She called me. I think she was trying to get me to rethink the divorce or something."

Megan sighed. "Typical. I don't think she understands the concept of divorce. They didn't have them in her day. I think they tried to work out their differences then and carry on. Or perhaps they just suffered in silence?"

Laura squirmed. "Look, I'll be off to the baby department. See you there, sweetie. Nice to meet you, Megan." She kissed Stephen on the cheek and hurried away.

Megan looked at her and wondered why Stephen had left her for someone so different in looks. Thin and angular, Laura's shape was the complete opposite of Megan's wide-hipped hourglass figure. Then those last words registered. "Baby department?" Megan enquired. "Is she—?"

It was Stephen's turn to look uncomfortable. "Yes."

"Congratulations."

"It was an accident."

Megan shrugged. "None of my concern, *sweetie*. Look, I have to go. Lots of things to do."

"Yes, but ... we need to sort this out. The house, I mean."

She stared at him. "Why? Oh, you think... you *hope* this happened before we split up? So that you can claim half the value?" She beamed an ironic smile at him. "Sorry to disappoint, but my Uncle Pat died only a month ago. Just after our divorce was finalised. And the whole thing is subject to probate, so I won't be the rightful owner until that's sorted out. Could take months." She waggled her fingers at him. "Byeee. Good luck with fatherhood. I hope it's twins." She turned on her heel and walked out of the department store.

Tears welling up, a hard knot in her chest, Megan half ran up the street to the tram station. *Pregnant, she's pregnant. Having his baby. Just like that. We discussed it for years, and every time he said he wouldn't, couldn't agree to start a family just yet. He wasn't ready. Wanted to think about it. Get his career to take off. Save some more money. Buy a bigger house. Wait for the economy to improve. Then she gets knocked up "by accident" and it's okay with him. And here I am, thirty-eight, divorced, childless and unemployed.*

She caught sight of her own reflection in a shop window and shuddered. Hopeless hair, tired face and bad posture, a shadow of the confident woman of not so long ago.

"Stand up straight," she heard a voice say behind her. "Blow your nose, and stop feeling sorry for yourself."

Startled, she looked around and discovered a woman with a girl in her early teens. Mother and daughter. The girl surly, the mother exasperated. Nothing to do with her. Certain it was a sign all the same, Megan pulled herself up both mentally and physically and continued up the street, telling herself she and nobody else was responsible for her life.

CHAPTER 3

Megan was packing the last few things when the phone rang. She picked up her mobile. "Hello?"

"Guess what?"

"Who's this?" She only faintly recognised the male voice and felt irritated at this interruption. She was moving out of her flat a few days later to live with her mother in the outer suburbs, a prospect she didn't relish. She had tried to get a new job but, despite being called to several interviews, received no offers. Her back up against a financial wall, she finally agreed to her mother's pleas of moving back home 'temporarily' and staying in her old room with Barbie wallpaper and the bed with a pink candlewick bedspread. The dream of the house in Kerry slowly faded with every passing week of no news. She resigned herself to the fact that she would either have to wait a year or more before she got possession, or not get it at all.

"Stop playing games and tell me who you are," she snapped. "I'm very busy."

"Okay, calm down," he laughed. "Sorry, I should have told you who I am first. It's just that I was so excited that…"

Megan now recognised the slight Kerry accent. Her heart skipped a beat. "Dan? Dan Nolan? Is that you? And you have some news? About the house?" Her knees shaking, she sank down on a chair. "Tell me, then."

He laughed again. "Okay. Are you sitting down? The probate's gone through. The house is yours."

Stunned, Megan sat there for a full minute before she could speak. "The house? It's mine? Really? Are you sure?"

"Of course I'm sure. I have the letter right here on my desk."

"That was quick."

"Yup, very quick. Two months. Must be some kind of record. So what are you going to do? Keep it? Sell it? Sell the land and keep the house?"

"I don't know," Megan said, her mind whirling. "I really don't. It's so sudden. I can't really take it in."

"Well, why don't you come down for the weekend and have a look at it again? Just so you know what kind of state it's in. The weather's good now, so you could do a little tour of the area. I can give you the name of a B and B nearby that's quite cheap."

"Okay," Megan mumbled. "I will."

"Great. See you Saturday," Dan said and hung up.

* * *

"*Born free,*" Megan sang at the top of her voice in duet with Andy Williams on the car radio, "*as free as the wind blows…*" The rush of it made her feel slightly dizzy so she closed the window and concentrated on the road. She was just coming into the cute little village of Adare with its ancient ruins, eleventh-century church and monastery. It was full of thatched cottages with little gardens adorned with roses and peonies, trendy restaurants and shops selling handcrafted pottery, and a long tail of cars and tourist buses. She sighed, stopping behind a German-registered Golf. Everyone and his mother seemed to want to go through Adare today. She opened the window again to let in the mild air. The weather had finally turned warm and sunny, a great relief from the chilly winds and drizzle of the past month—more like January than June.

After the call from Dan, Megan phoned her mother to say she wasn't moving in right away but was departing to Kerry for a week or two. With the exception of her red sofa and the antique desk her father had bought for her thirtieth birthday, her furniture went to a second-hand shop. The remaining items were stored in her mother's garage to be claimed once she had found suitable accommodation on her return to Dublin.

All she had was a suitcase with her clothes, a box full of shoes and her laptop. *Talk about minimalist*, she said to herself, realising that having very few possessions was liberating rather than frightening. Megan felt, yet again, a dart of happiness as she thought of the adventure ahead. She had no actual plan and no idea what she was going to do once she got to Kerry except collect the keys and the deeds to the house.

"Next stop, The Blue Door B and B," she muttered, as the traffic started to move again. Probably your typical Irish guest house with cutesy décor aimed at American tourists. A hostess called Mairead or Kathleen, who would be chatting about the weather and ask if she wanted the 'full Irish' for breakfast. Well, she could put up with that for a while.

* * *

The door of The Blue Door was red. Megan rang the bell of the white stucco house, where hanging baskets crammed with geraniums adorned the façade.

No reply. She rang again, then pushed at the door, peering into the deserted wood panelled hall. She tiptoed in and put her suitcase on the floor.

"Hello?" Her voice echoed up the wide staircase. There was a faint smell of fried sausages and smouldering briquettes. A smell she remembered from staying in B and B's in her childhood. She hadn't stayed in such a place since then, boutique hotels being her preferred accommodation when on holiday. She thought fleetingly of spa hotels, of sinking into a pool somewhere in the sun but pushed the thought away. She had to live for the moment, not yearn for those halcyon days of a job and an expense account.

A door flung open. A thin woman with light-blonde hair in a ponytail, wearing tight jeans and an orange tee-shirt, rushed into the hall. "Hello. Sorry, I was outside taking in the laundry, so I didn't hear you." She spoke with the hard R's and thick L's of an East European accent. She studied Megan through pale blue eyes. "Have you booked a room?"

Megan smiled and nodded. "Yes, I just arrived. I booked a single room for the weekend."

The woman held out her hand. "Hello and welcome. I'm Beata."

"Hello, I'm Megan O'Farrell. Um, but—"

"Yes?"

"I was going to ask why you call this place The Blue Door when it's red. The door, I mean."

Beata shrugged. "They were out of blue at the hardware store, but we had to stick with the name because everyone knows it. Anything else?"

"No."

"Good. I'll show you to your room." Beata raced up the stairs and down the corridor at breakneck speed with Megan at her heels. She flung open a door. "Here's your room. The keys are in the door. Breakfast between eight and ten tomorrow morning. Have a good stay."

Megan fought for air. "Okay. Thanks. Could you just tell me where I might get something to eat around here?"

Beata hovered on the threshold. "Mulligans. Out on the

Maharees. It's a pub, but they have great food too. If you have nothing better to do tonight, maybe you'd like to join Boris and me when we go out there later?"

"Boris? Your husband?"

Beata let out a snort. "You think I'd marry a Russian? Nah, he's okay to ride but marry him? No way."

Megan blinked. "Uh, I see…"

"So how about it?"

"Why not? Thanks, I'd love to."

"Good. See you downstairs at seven. You'll love their food. They do great fish." Beata rushed out of the room and banged the door shut.

Megan put the suitcase on a chair and looked around the sparsely furnished room. A double bed with a colourful quilt and many cushions. A bedside table. Two easy chairs and a long padded seat by the window overlooking the bay. Everything painted a distressed white, even the floorboards with a Scandinavian look. Stark but peaceful.

No time to linger. She had stopped off at the solicitor's office when she passed through Tralee. A chirpy receptionist handed her an envelope with 'keys and deeds, as instructed'.

Megan pulled the envelope out of her tote bag and took out the deeds. It gave her a thrill to see her name as the owner of the house at 'Kilshee, County Kerry'. The keys were old and rusty. *My house*, she thought and stuffed them into the pocket of her shorts. She changed her sandals for running shoes, pulled on a sweatshirt and was ready to take possession of her new home.

* * *

The house looked exactly the same. Megan got out of the car, banged the door shut and jumped over the broken fence.

She squinted at the mountains in the afternoon sun, listened happily to the gurgle of the stream and breathed in sweet, salt-scented air. Not wanting to tackle the inside of the house just yet, she sank down on the back step.

She closed her eyes, enjoying the sun on her face and felt a calm come over her, just like the last time. She exhaled with a contented sigh.

Like a knife ripping the canvas of a beautiful painting, a loud rumble broke the silence. Megan shot up from the step. Looking wildly around, she saw the back of a trailer come into view. *What the—*? She rushed around the side of the house and stared at the tractor with a large trailer full of bellowing calves backing in through the gate.

The tractor stopped. A scruffy man jumped out. He froze when he caught sight of Megan. "What are you doing here?" he demanded in a sing-song Kerry accent.

"I'm…" Megan stammered. "This is my…"

"What?" The man said. "I'm loading off these calves, so you'd better get out of the way. In any case, this is private property."

Megan pulled herself up. "I know this is private property. It's *my* private property, as a matter of fact. So if anyone's trespassing, it's you."

The man blinked. "Come again?"

She took a deep breath. "I own this house and… and the… land thereof. My Uncle Pat willed it to me when he died. I mean, he put me in his will before he died."

The man took off his cap and scratched his thatch of black hair. His bright-blue eyes studied her for a long time. "Who are you then? Sean's daughter?"

Megan nodded. "Yes. I'm Megan O'Farrell."

"Thought so. You look like him. With his red hair and brown eyes. So Pat gave his house to you?" He started to laugh. "The crafty bastard."

"What do you mean?"

"Long story."

Megan studied him. Tall and broad-shouldered, dressed in scruffy jeans and a sweater full of holes, he was an attractive man despite his unshaven, messy appearance. He looked back at her with a glint of approval and something else she couldn't quite decipher.

"Who are you?" she demanded. "And what are you doing here?"

He wiped his hand on the back of his jeans and held it out. "Sorry. Where are my manners? I'm Paudie O'Shea."

His big hand was rough and calloused, his grip firm. Their eyes met for an instant, before Megan withdrew her hand and dropped her gaze. "Hello," was all she managed. She looked at him again. "Uh, I don't think I want your calves in my garden. And—" Her eyes drifted to the sheep grazing on the other side of the fence. "Are those your sheep?"

"Yup."

"And the cows on the other side?"

"No."

She suspected he was laughing at her. "No? Whose are they, then?"

"Mine. But they're not cows, they're bullocks."

"Okay. Whatever." Megan shifted from one leg to the other. "I don't care if they're giraffes, they're on my land, and you don't have permission to—"

He glared at her. "Well, I'm sorry to upset your little applecart here, but the land has been let to me as conacre."

"Who's Con Acre? Never heard of him."

"Have you never heard of conacre?"

"I don't think we've been introduced, no."

"It's not a he. It's a kind of contract. Hiring land for tillage or grazing. Conacre. Very well-known term."

"Oh," Megan said, deflated. "Okay. Right. But that must have been an arrangement you made with my... the previous owner."

"You bet it was. An arrangement that goes back to my granddad's time. He and Pat were great pals."

"So?"

"So I've paid in full for this year. Two hundred euros an acre. And the contract is good for another ten years. At least."

"Oh. Right." Megan took a step back. "I'll have to check that with my solicitor."

Paudie shrugged. "Check away. Now, I have work to do, so if you'll excuse me ... " He started to walk around the back of the trailer.

Megan trotted after him. "No, you don't. You might have the right to the land on the other side of the fence, but I bet you don't have any right to graze cattle in my garden."

He stopped dead. "What are you going to do? Call the Guards?"

Megan folded her arms. "Yes. I will if you don't get out of my garden."

He sighed. "You're a stubborn girl, aren't you? Just like your uncle."

"You bet I am." Megan hauled her phone out of her bag. "Get that tractor out of my garden, or I'll call the Guards."

"Yeah, right." He started to open the back of the trailer.

Megan punched 999 into her phone. "I'm calling them right now."

Paudie looked up. "That's one helluva smart phone. I mean, you're able to talk into it without switching it on."

"What? Oh." Megan felt her face redden. She looked at her phone. "Shit." Tears of anger and frustration blurred her vision. She put her phone away.

His eyes softened. "Listen, I'll just leave the calves here for two days, while I spray my fields up there at the farm. Then I'll come and take them away and I won't bother you again. How's that?"

Megan backed away. "No. I don't want your cattle in my

garden." She picked up her phone again and switched it on. "I'm going to call my solicitor."

He played with the catch on the trailer's ramp. Then, without another word, stomped back to the tractor and started the engine. "Good luck finding Dan Nolan on a Saturday," he shouted over the rumble before he took off.

"Good luck to you too." Megan mumbled, closing the gate.

CHAPTER 4

Mulligan's pub was flooded with the golden light of the late evening sun. A stone-faced, low building, it had wonderful views of Brandon bay and the mountains beyond. Far out at sea, waves crashed against the rocks of an island. The sails of two windsurfers bouncing on the waves were just visible.

Megan closed the door of Beata's ancient van. "How beautiful."

"Not bad," Beata agreed. "Come on, Boris, get your ass out of the car. I need a drink."

The tall Russian scrambled out of the back seat. "Okay. Don't twist your panties." He smiled amiably at Megan. "She takes no prisoners."

Megan laughed. "No, so I gather." She had liked him instantly. A handsome man with high cheekbones and features that seemed to have been hewn out of a rock, he had dark, nearly black eyes and a thatch of brown hair. "I'd say she has a good heart, though."

He nodded. "A good, warm heart with much kindness." He put his finger to his lips. "But, shh, she no want anyone to know."

"Your English is getting worse instead of better," Beata remarked. "Could you try to keep that gob shut tonight? I don't need to be embarrassed again like the last time. Nobody wants to hear the details of our sex life. Or how big my boobs are."

"Yes, boss." Boris shuffled into the pub.

"He's such an arsehole sometimes." Beata sighed. "But strong as an ox and very useful to have around when something needs fixing. Must work on his English, though. Can't have him using language like that."

"Uh, no," Megan started. "You have an interesting turn of phrase yourself."

Beata's eyes turned colder than a glacier. "I'm from Poland, in case you were wondering. I've been here a long time, and Ireland isn't the land of the welcomes but a lot better than a small village in the middle of Poland. And I'm not the maid of the Blue Door but the owner." She drew breath.

Megan squirmed. "I didn't think—"

"Yes you did. Everyone does. 'Where are you from? Have you been here long?' That's what you were going to ask, wasn't it? Then you assumed I was the maid. I could see that's exactly what was going through your mind."

"No, it wasn't. I was going to ask how come you speak such good English."

"I learned English from my dad. He was a seaman and worked on English trawlers for years."

"That explains your, uh, fluency."

"Thanks. Let's go in. I could kill for a drink."

The noise in the pub was a sharp contrast to the peace outside, where the silence was only broken by the plaintive cry of a seagull. Inside, the chatter of many voices, loud music and a large TV screen, showing a soccer match, brought Megan back to Dublin. But the sweaters and jeans, deep tans and tousled hair of the crowd were different from pub-goers in the city. You could tell most of these people had been out surfing or sailing all day. In her sequined tee-shirt, tight, short skirt and high heels, she didn't exactly blend in. She looked around, but Beata and Boris had disappeared into the crowd. She elbowed herself to the bar and ordered a glass of Guinness.

Someone jostled her as she picked up her glass. "Sorry! Oh, Megan?"

She turned around. Confused, she tried to place him. "Hi, uh, Dan."

In tee-shirt and shorts, his hair damp, he looked younger than the solicitor she had met two months earlier. "Hi. Nice to see you again."

"Yes, great. You've been swimming?"

He pushed his hair back. "No, surfing. Some great waves today. So you decided to come and spend the weekend?"

She suddenly felt self-conscious. "Yes... I mean... no, I thought I'd stay around for a bit."

"Oh, yes. So you said."

"I'm staying at the Blue Door." A thought struck her. "Listen, there's a bit of a problem with my... with the land and stuff. I tried to call you earlier but there was no reply."

He laughed. "Yeah, well, the surf was up, so I was busy catching a wave."

"I see. But now that you're here, maybe you could explain something to me?"

He lifted a bushy black eyebrow. "Okay, let me get a drink, and we can have a chat about it." He turned to the bartender. "A pint of lager, please." He smiled at Megan and gestured to an empty spot at the bar further away. "'Let's grab those seats."

"Okay." Megan inched her way along the bar and sat down.

Perched on a stool, Dan raised his pint of lager. "Cheers and good luck with your new property. So what was it you wanted to ask me?"

Megan sipped her Guinness. "I had a bit of a problem with a farmer today. Paudie something, I think his name was. He seems to be renting my fields in something called conacre, which you seem to have forgotten to mention."

"But I did."

Megan frowned. "No, I don't remember that."

"Probably because you were half asleep."

"Must have been while you were droning on about property laws. I kind of lost interest halfway through. Maybe you should improve your reading skills? Make it more interesting so your clients don't fall asleep."

He put his glass on the counter. "You mean you expect it to be some sort of entertainment? I'm sorry if I bored you, but I thought, as it concerned your property, you might have made an attempt to stay awake."

"I didn't know I had a property at that stage. You might have told me that at the beginning and then—" Megan stopped. "Aren't we losing track of the real issue here?"

"Yes." He took another swig. "What was the issue?"

"Paudie O'Shea and his conacre. He said the contract was good for ten years."

Dan shook his head. "No, it's not. It's renewable at the end of every year. He's paid until then, and after that it's up to you if you want to continue."

"But he has the right to put cattle in the garden too? He tried to unload some calves."

"No, absolutely not. He probably took the liberty, thinking there was nobody around. I suspect your Uncle Pat said it was okay or something. You have to sort that out with Paudie."

"Or you could write him a letter," Megan suggested.

"Could do. But if you speak to him first, he might agree without much pressure."

Megan sighed. "I doubt that very much."

Dan winked. "But a pretty face goes much further than a solicitor's letter."

She smiled stiffly. "Of course. That's what I always use. My charm and femininity."

"Thought so." He winked. "You have foam on your lip."

She wiped it off. "Thanks."

"You're welcome."

"What'll I do about Paudie?"

Dan drained his glass. "Nothing for the moment. Let me know if he causes any trouble, and I'll go and beat him up."

"Very funny." Megan wriggled off her stool. "Goodbye." She took her half-finished glass and pushed into the crowd, looking for Beata or Boris.

Someone touched her arm. A stocky, red-haired man in his fifties blocked her way. "Are you the O'Farrell girl?"

"Um, yes?"

His beady eyes studied her for a moment. "Thought so. You've that O'Farrell look. He grabbed her hand so roughly, she nearly dropped her glass. "Tom Quinn. Your Aunt Molly's nephew."

Megan took a step back. "Hello. Nice to meet you."

He looked at her in silence for a moment. "So, how did you do it, then?"

"Do what?"

"Get him to will you the house."

"I don't know what you mean."

The man grabbed her arm. "We were very good to Pat the last few years. Worked hard we did, for him. Helped him with the animals, drove him to the shops, even dug the potatoes. Hard work it was. My brother and I went to see him nearly every day in the nursing home. And he swore we would get the place when he died." He moved closer still. "But a pretty girl like you wouldn't have any trouble getting an old man to part with his property," he wheezed in her ear. He smelled of sweat and beer.

Megan pulled away. "I really—" They were interrupted by a voice calling for Megan.

Beata sidled up to them. "Come over and meet our friends." She nodded at Tom Quinn. "Hi. I'm Beata."

He smirked. "Yeah, I've seen you before. Not from around

here are you?"

Beata frowned. "No. From Poland."

Tom nodded. "Yes, thought so. A blow-in."

Beata bristled. "What do you take me for? I don't do stuff like that." She pulled at Megan. "Come on, we don't want to talk to this fucker."

Tom Quinn lifted his glass. "Have a nice evening, ladies."

"Bastard," Beata growled when they were at the door. "Did you hear what he called me? A 'blow-in'. As if... I mean..."

Megan took Beata's arm. "Hey. Listen, it's not what you think." She struggled to keep her face straight. "A 'blow-in' means a stranger. Someone who's not from here. Have you never heard it before?"

Beata's jaw dropped. "Oh... I see. I thought he meant some kind of tart giving—you know..."

Megan let out a giggle. "Yeah, I know what you thought."

" Oh shit. Thanks for letting me know. But that guy's still a fucker. I've seen him around. Always getting drunk and touching up women."

They were interrupted by a shrill sound from Megan's bag. She put her glass on a nearby table and fished out her phone. "Hello?"

A voice said something she couldn't hear. "Hang on. I'm in a pub. Can't hear a thing. I'll go outside. Sorry," she said to Beata. "Phone call." She inched her way through the crowd and walked to the door. Once outside, she put the phone to her ear. "Okay. Can hear you now."

The male voice said something in a Kerry accent so thick, it was impossible to understand more than '—on the road'.

Megan pressed the phone harder to her ear. "What? On the road? Could you speak more slowly? Who is this?"

"Mick Ryan. I live down the road from your house."

"What?" Megan asked, confused. "How did you get my

number?"

"Dan Nolan gave it to me. Said it would be useful in case something happened. And now it has. Your cattle are on the road."

"What cattle?" Megan looked wildly around and was relieved to see Beata, coming out of the pub, puffing on a cigarette. "Hang on, I'll put you on to my friend who understands the language." She handed the phone to Beata. "Here. Please try to find out what's going on. I don't speak Kerry."

Without removing the cigarette, Beata took the phone. "Hey, what's your problem? You harassing this woman, huh?" She listened for a moment, then: "What the fuck do you mean? Megan doesn't have any cattle. You must have the wrong number. If you don't stop this, I'll call the—"

The voice grew louder.

"What's going on?" Megan hissed, trying to take the phone.

Beata puffed on her cigarette "I see. Okay. I'll tell her. We'll be right over." She handed the phone to Megan. "He says there are cattle on the road outside your house. You have a house?"

"Yes. Just an old wreck I inherited. Don't really know what to do with it. Then today this guy with a trailer arrived trying to unload some calves into the garden, but I told him I'd call the police so he left. Must have snuck back later when I was gone and unloaded them."

"Who was he?"

Megan shrugged. "Said his name was Paudie O'Shea."

Beata's eyes narrowed. "I see…"

"You know him?"

"Yes, sure I do. Creep."

"What am I going to do?"

Beata marched to her van. "Get in. We'll sort this out."

Megan got into the passenger seat. "What about Boris?"

Beata slid behind the wheel and slammed the door shut.

"We'll leave him here. He's drunk. No use to anyone."

"Where are we going?" Megan asked when the van took off.

Beata squinted through the cigarette smoke. "First, we'll go to the house and see about the cattle. Then we'll go and have a little chat with Paudie."

"It's very kind of you to help."

Beata laughed. "Kind? I've been waiting for a reason to stick it to that bastard for a year."

* * *

Four calves grazed on the sparse grass at the edge of the lane. Beata stopped the van. "There they are. All together. Great. This won't be too hard."

"What are we going to do?" Megan asked.

Beata smirked. "We're going to drive them back up to Paudie. It's not far. A couple of kilometres up the lane."

"How?"

"On foot, of course." Beata glanced at Megan's shoes. " Oh shit. Your shoes are useless. And that miniskirt's pathetic. You have fantastic legs, but that won't help you now. Hey, there's a pair of willies in the van. Stick those on and we're away."

"You mean wellies, I hope?"

"Yeah, whatever. Willies, wellies, same difference."

"Uh, not quite." Megan found a pair of muddy boots in the back of the van. She pulled them on and tossed in her stilettos. "How's that?" she called, walking around the car.

Beata laughed. "Not the most elegant look but better for this job." She glanced at the house. "This is it? This wreck?"

"Yes. The house my great-uncle left me in his will."

Beata looked around. "Good location. That beach is great for surfing. Lovely mountain views, and straight up that road you have some good hiking trails. But the house needs a lot of work, if you're planning to live there."

Megan shrugged. "I know. But I don't want to think about that now."

"You're right. None of my earwax anyway. Come on, let's go. Grab that stick over there and get behind the little fuckers. I'll go to the side to stop them getting in through the hedges. Let's go." She let out an ear-splitting holler. The calves jumped to attention. "Woo, woo, woo!" she shouted, waving her arms. "Come on, you bastards, get going up the road."

Megan waved her stick, pushing the calves ahead. The wellies chafed her ankles, making her wobble. The calves scattered all over the road, and she had trouble keeping them together. But Beata managed to get them in line.

They walked slowly up the lane lined with wildflowers and fuchsia. The sun sank lower behind the mountains. Birdsong, the buzzing of bees and the soft bellowing of the calves made a pleasant, mellow symphony. Megan waved her stick, occasionally calling to the calves and began to enjoy the summer's evening adventure.

She waved away a fly. "So, why do you hate Paudie so much?"

"He's a two-faced bastard."

"What did he do?"

Beata whacked at a bush. "Oh, nothing much. We had this thing going, you know?"

"Yeah?"

Beata looked into the distance. "I had just arrived here. I was lonely. Not used to… men. Paudie was so cute. So flirty. I thought he was only interested in me but of course, he's like that with all women."

"Not with me," Megan remarked "He was anything but flirty earlier today."

"That's unusual." Beata tapped at the back of a calf with her stick. "Go on, move!" She slowed down again. "Well anyway, I fell in love with him, I suppose. I never met someone like that. A small village in Poland isn't crawling with handsome hunks, you know."

"No, I can imagine." Beata's downcast expression made Megan feel a sudden sympathy. "I'm sure you were homesick too. That can make you fall for the wrong men, I'm sure."

"Homesick? For a village in the middle of nowhere? Where there's no work and everyone is dirt-poor? No way. But I missed my family, of course."

"I'm sure you did."

"Then I met Paudie. I looked into his baby-blue eyes and fell for him big time. We were in bed the very first night we met. I don't think we actually said much, except 'hello, how are you?' Just jumped into bed. Didn't get out of it for two days. I was exhausted. God, that man knows how to fuck!"

Megan squirmed. "Uh, really?"

Beata giggled. "Sorry. That was a little too much information, wasn't it?"

"Just a tad. But I know what you mean. Some men are like that. They get under your skin. Addictive or something."

Beata glanced sideways at Megan. "You've been there too?"

Megan nodded. "Yeah. Bad marriage. He left me for a younger model. You know. Skinny. Shiny hair. Gorgeous face. The usual."

"Shit. I'm sorry. How long were you married?"

"Eight years. It was good, I thought. I loved him. Thought he loved me. We had great sex. No idea what that bimbo could offer that I couldn't. And now she's pregnant. Something he didn't manage with me. But never mind about that. Go on with your story."

"No, I want to hear more about you," Beata said. "Not the bad marriage but what you did as a living and how you came to inherit the house."

Megan slowed her pace. "I was what you call a stylist. Which means you help people dress the right way. But to me, that wasn't all there was too it."

Beata looked at her with interest. "Really? I thought stylists were the kind of people who got celebrities to look glam on the red carpet."

Megan laughed. "Yes, that's if you live in Hollywood. But I worked with normal people. Sometimes I had newly elected politicians as my clients. Or high-powered executives. Or the wives of executives, who needed to look their best in the public eye. Often women with low self-esteem and not much confidence. You've no idea what a little polish and the right outfit can do to give them a lift."

"I'm sure it does. Must be difficult to handle really ugly people with no style. I could never do that."

"Not always easy," Megan agreed. "But everyone has something attractive about them, so you point out the good bits and then carefully tell them how to hide the bad bits."

Beata stopped. "So, what about me? What would you say if I asked you to improve my look?"

Megan forgot about the calves and studied Beata. "Um… you have a great figure and good skin." She hesitated. She was going to say that sticking your head in a bucket of bleach was not the right way to go blonde and that all the black eye make-up made her look more than cheap, but the look in those pale blue eyes was too intimidating.

"But? I hear a 'but' there."

"Well, maybe orange isn't the best colour on someone with such pale skin? Something softer might bring out your blue eyes. But I wouldn't touch anything else," Megan added. "Except perhaps adding a bit of blusher or something. But that's a minor thing."

"Hmm." Beata didn't look satisfied. "That's not the whole story is it? I'm sure there's a whole lot more wrong with me, but you're too chicken to tell me."

"No," Megan protested. "Not at all. Of course, if we got into the nit-picking stage, I might point out other things. But on the whole, the thing about you is that you have a great personality. You make me laugh. And you look like the kind of person I'd want to know better. That's not about hair or clothes, it's about aura. And you have a nice one."

Beata put her arm through Megan's. "You have a very nice aura, too."

Megan started walking again. "So what about you and Paudie? What happened?

Beata shrugged. "Not much to tell. We had a few months together. I moved into his house. But then we started to fight, and one day he just threw me out."

Megan stopped and stared at Beata. "He threw you out? What a bastard."

"Yeah. So now you know why I want to get back at him."

"Yes, and so do I." Megan waved her stick again and increased her pace, pushing the calves ahead of her up the road.

Everything was going smoothly, until one of the calves crashed through a hedge into a field.

"Shit!" Beata shouted. "Go after him, Megan. I have to keep these ones on the road."

Megan squeezed through the hedge, the brambles scratching her arms, into the field, trying to get around the gambolling calf. He kicked out. She ducked and fell into a fresh cowpat.

Beata screamed with laughter. "Get up, quick, he's getting away!"

Megan scrambled to her feet and ran after the calf, waving her stick. She managed to get behind him, turn him around and finally back onto the road.

Beata couldn't stop laughing. Gasping for breath, she herded the calves on. "I'm sorry but you looked so funny. It was like something from Father Ted."

Megan pushed her hair out of her eyes. "Yeah, right. Ha,

ha."

Beata calmed down. "I'm sorry about your clothes. But the skirt can be washed and the top... well, we can pick the cow shit out of the sequins and wash it by hand."

Megan pulled the top away from her body. "I'll never wear it again. God, it stinks."

"You could always take it off."

"And go around naked? A great first impression that'd make."

"Sorry. Of course. Look, here we are. Paudie's place."

Megan stopped. The house was long and low, painted white with a slate roof. A concrete courtyard in front with a tractor parked outside the door. Geraniums in a wooden tub added a dash of colour to the otherwise drab entrance. A big, black dog of indistinguishable breed lifted his head from his paws and let out a soft 'woof'.

"Nice house," Megan remarked.

"Yes, it's okay." Beata looked around. "Now, where can we put these calves? Where would it be most annoying?"

"In the hay barn?" Megan suggested. "Then they'd eat hay that's intended for next winter."

"Hmm, yes. That could work. Or—" Beata walked to a gate. "Aha! Cows. Let's put them in there. That must be the mummies. He must have just weaned the babies, judging by the bellowing and mooing."

They swiftly ushered the calves into the field, where they galloped off to join the cows coming toward them.

The dog barked. The door flew open and Paudie rushed out. "What's going on? Who opened the gate and let those calves in?"

The cattle's bellowing and the dog's barking mingled into an ear-splitting cacophony. Megan put her hands over her ears.

"Shut up!" Beata shouted. "Down, Denis!" The dog whimpered and slunk away.

When all was quiet, Paudie drew breath. "Would you mind telling me what's going on here?"

"We brought your calves back," Megan said. "They seemed to be lost."

"Yeah," Beata said. "They missed their mummies."

Paudie stared at them. "What? Would you mind saying that again?"

Megan drew breath. "You had the nerve to put those calves in my garden when my back was turned. A neighbour called to tell me they had broken loose and were on the road. He thought they were mine."

"So, yeah, we thought we'd help you out a little," Beata said. "Get those calves back where they came from."

Paudie looked at the field, where the calves were trying to feed from the cows. "There's a slight problem with that, though."

Megan glared at him. "And what would that be?"

"Those are not my calves."

Beata's jaw dropped. "What? Not your—"

Paudie shook his head. "Nope. I put mine in the yard behind the barn. It's not ideal, but as I had nowhere else to put them while I wait for the field I sprayed to be safe, I had to park them somewhere."

"Shit," Beata said.

Megan pushed back her hair. "But whose are they?"

Paudie looked at her as if he had just noticed she was there. "I didn't recognise you at first. Megan, isn't it?"

"Yes."

He studied her with an amused expression. "You look lovely tonight. Going on somewhere, are we?"

Megan pulled at her top. "I had to chase the calves through a hedge, and then I fell into a—"

He sniffed. "Yes, I can tell."

"What are we going to do?" Beata said.

Paudie shrugged. "I'm going to go back in to finish my

tea. I suggest you get the calves out of there and back down the road. I think they must belong to the Connolly-Smiths on the main road. They'll be rather miffed about this." He started to walk back to the house. "Tell Jack I said hello."

"Shit." Beata looked at Megan. "Oh, please, don't cry."

Megan blinked away tears. "Sorry. I'm just so tired and fed up."

"This is all my fault," Beata moaned. "I'm so sorry."

"You were just trying to help."

Paudie stopped by the door. He looked back at them and sighed. "Okay, come in, girls. We'll sort it out. And I'll give you a clean tee-shirt if you want to get out of that mucky one, Megan."

"No," Beata said. "I'm not going inside that house ever again."

Paudie opened the door. "Suit yourselves."

Megan hovered between solidarity to Beata and a clean tee-shirt. She took a deep breath. "Hang on. I'm coming."

Paudie held the door open as she approached. "After you, your ladyship."

"Abandon all hope, ye who enter here," Beata muttered darkly from the gate.

CHAPTER 5

A sharp contrast to the drab exterior, the inside of Paudie's house revealed astonishing sophistication and artistic flair. Waiting for him to get her the promised tee-shirt from the bedroom, Megan looked around the living room.

The traditional farmhouse layout had been altered to knock two rooms together into one bright, inviting space. Colourful rugs lay on the wooden floor, a big chintz sofa with cushions and a mohair throw stood by the window. Two leather armchairs flanked the stove. A large pine sideboard at the far wall, where ceramic bowls and framed photos caught the sunshine pouring in through sash windows.

Pictures, posters and paintings hung in haphazard disarray on whitewashed walls, each one beautiful and intriguing with a common theme: nature.

Lost in a big poster depicting a mountain range with breathtaking views, Megan jumped when Paudie came into the room.

He tossed a tee-shirt at her. "Here. Put this on. You can put the other one in a plastic bag."

Megan held up the tee-shirt. "I 'heart' Boston?"

"Yeah. Someone gave it to me when I left."

"You were in Boston?"

"Yes. Spent five years there. Worked in an Irish pub, then did a course. Ended up in Vermont, teaching. Great place."

"And you 'hearted' it?"

He laughed. "Yes, kinda."

"So why did you come back?"

He shrugged. "Long story. Do you want to change in the bathroom? It's through there on the other side of the hall."

"Thanks."

In the bathroom, Megan laughed at the muddy boots on the floor, the grimy towels and faint ring around the bathtub. Someone didn't have his priorities right.

She carefully stripped off the smelly top and threw it on the floor. The tee-shirt, both big and wide, slipped down to her hips. It was a relief to wear something smelling of soap instead of cow shit. She kicked the soiled top under the sink. Sighing, she turned to the mirror and tried to smooth her tangled hair. Having rubbed the smudges off her face with the corner of a reasonably clean facecloth, she was satisfied she had done her best and returned to the living room. Finding it deserted, she walked through an open door into the kitchen, where she discovered Paudie making tea at the stove.

Unlike the living room, the kitchen was cluttered and untidy. But with the smell of newly baked bread and the warmth of the big stove, it was cosy and inviting. The checked curtains, scarred pine table and tiled floor added to a lived-in feel. A dresser crammed with mugs, plates and stacks of newspapers filled an entire wall. A farmer's calendar, postcards and snapshots were pinned to a noticeboard.

Paudie offered her a mug. "Tea?"

"Thanks." Megan took the mug. She removed a pile of sweaters and shirts from a chair and sat down.

Paudie joined her. "Tee-shirt okay?"

"Yes, thanks. It's too big but lovely and clean."

He got up. "I'll get you the dirty one."

Megan put a hand on his arm. "No, it's okay. You can throw it in the bin. I don't think I'll ever want to wear it again."

"All right." He pushed a plate across the table. "Pizza. Cold now, but still okay. You want a piece?"

Megan picked up a wedge. "Oh, thanks. I haven't eaten since lunchtime. I'm starving."

He helped himself too and they munched in silence.

Megan wiped her mouth. "Thanks. I needed that."

"Okay. Listen, I called the Connolly-Smiths. They're sending up the lads with a trailer to get the calves. Once we have that sorted, I can drive you back to your house."

"What about Beata?"

He shrugged. "She left. Saw her walk down the road."

"Oh. But… I came in her van, so if she drove off, I'll have to walk back to Castlegregory. I'm staying at The Blue Door, you see."

"I'll drive you over." He pushed a bread basket at her. "Here. Some fresh soda bread."

"You baked it?"

"Ha, ha, no. I get it in Lidl in Tralee. Then I warm it in the oven. There is a limit to my talents."

Remembering Beata's words about his talents, Megan blushed. She took another slice of pizza and nibbled on it. Paudie slurped his tea. A grey cat padded in through the half-open door and slunk around their legs, meowing. Paudie poured some milk on a saucer and put it on the floor. The cat lapped it up, then sat back and started to clean itself.

There was an awkward silence, as Megan tried to think of something to say. "What you said earlier… about Uncle Pat and him leaving the house to me…"

"What did I say?"

"You said 'the crafty bastard' and laughed your head off."

Paudie nodded. "Yeah, that made me laugh. Thought that was very funny. Everyone wondered who'd get the farm and the bit of land. They were all bending over backwards to please him the last few years. But the old fox never let on. So he made a will, did he?"

"Yes."

"Well, I'll be…" Paudie chuckled. "The Quinns will choke on their porridge when they find out."

"Who are the Quinns?" Megan demanded. "And why will they choke?"

"Molly's family. They thought they'd get the house and the bit of land. Always going around saying Pat had promised them. Ha. He fooled them until the very end. And Dan Nolan knew this all along, I bet. Never said a word."

"Why would he?"

"Indeed," Paudie said. "Why would he? Probably had great fun knowing about it and watching the Quinns suck up to Pat. Anyway, none of my business. Glad he willed it to you and not those ugly mugs." He looked at her thoughtfully. "What are you going to do with it?"

Megan found she didn't want to talk about her plans to Paudie. "I don't know yet."

As if sensing her discomfort, he changed the subject. "So, you're a friend of Beata?"

"No, we only just met today. She invited me to go to the pub and then, when I heard about the calves, she offered to help."

"Some help. Great opportunity for her to cause me trouble."

"Yes. I didn't realise that's what she was up to. But it had something to do with your relationship a while back. None of my business, I know but she said—"

Paudie put his mug down with a bang. "You know the saying about 'what happens in Vegas, stays in Vegas'?"

"Yes?"

"Same thing applies here. I'm not going to ask you about your sex life, so you stay out of mine, okay?"

Megan blushed. "I wasn't going to—"

He glared at her. "Like hell you weren't. Women are all the

same. Poking into everybody's love life and trying to analyse everything. Then they think they have all the answers, and before you know it, they've moved in and are tidying up your sock drawer and making you eat healthy food."

Megan blinked. "Where did that come from? We've only just met. Why would I be the slightest bit interested in you?"

His eyes softened. "Sorry. I'm a little bit touchy about that subject. Look, you and I should get on. We're related after all."

"We are?"

He nodded. "Yes. Only by marriage. Your Aunt Molly was my grandfather's sister."

Megan laughed. "That's amazing. Then you're related to a man I met in the pub tonight. Tom Quinn."

"Tom? Yeah, my mother's cousin. But we're not too fond of each other, and that's putting it mildly. He's one of those Quinns I told you about."

"I didn't take to him. He was quite nasty, but I think he was drunk."

Paudie nodded. "Very likely. He'll be as mad as hell he didn't get the house. He and his brother were smooching old Pat the last year or so. But he was clever enough to take what they offered and then do what he wanted all along—give the farm to Sean's daughter. The two of them must be livid. I'd stay away from them if I were you."

"Don't worry. I intend to."

He held out his hand. "Friends, then 'cousin'?"

"Of course." She took his rough, calloused hand. "Not quite cousins, so yes, friends. Sounds good to me."

He put his other hand over hers. "Friendship is better than love. Lasts longer."

"Absolutely." She looked into his bright blue eyes. "I'm off men at the moment, anyway."

He let go of her hand. "That makes two of us."

She giggled. "You're off men, too?"

"I'm off everybody, girl. I've had a rough year."

"Me too."

"You have?"

"Yeah. Bad marriage. Divorce. That sort of thing."

"That's tough." He touched her shoulder. "If you want someone to talk to, I'll listen."

"I think I'll leave that one in Vegas too, for the moment."

"Of course."

A rumble outside cut into the silence. Paudie got up. "I'll go and help the lads get the calves. Then I'll drive you over to the B and B."

Megan rose. "I'll tidy up the cups."

He winked. "Thanks. But leave my sock drawer alone, will you?"

* * *

Three battered vans loaded with surfboards stood outside The Blue Door when Paudie's jeep pulled up in the drive.

"Beata must have some new guests," Megan said.

Paudie leaned over and opened the door for her. "Surfers. They're here for the competition tomorrow."

"I see." Megan got out of the car. "Thanks for the lift and the tee-shirt. I'll bring it back later."

"No problem. See you soon, love." Paudie slammed the door and drove off.

The hall was piled with bags and wetsuits. Three men enjoyed a cup of tea in front of the fire in the sitting room. Megan nearly crashed into Beata coming out of the kitchen with a loaded tray.

"Oh, there you are. Still alive then? No obvious cuts and bruises I see."

Megan laughed. "No, he was perfectly civilised. Drove

me home."

"He must be feeling sick or something." Beata pushed the tray at Megan. "Could you bring this in? I have to make some more sandwiches."

Megan took the tray. "Okay. Who are they? Did you know they were coming?"

Beata sighed. "Yes, I did, but I forgot it was this weekend. And Boris is still in the pub, so I'm all alone. He'll stagger home sometime after midnight, I'm sure, and vomit on the cat and fall asleep in the kitchen. So I really need a little help here."

"Of course. I'll bring this in, and then I'll go and change my clothes. What else is there to do?"

"Just making ten beds and putting clean towels in the bathrooms," Beata groaned.

"Okay. I'll help you with that."

"Thanks. You're a star."

Megan carried the tray into the living room. "More tea?" she said.

One of the men got up. "I'll help you with that." Deeply tanned, his hair was bleached nearly white by sun and salt.

"Thanks." Megan gave him the tray. "Was that an Aussie accent I heard?"

"You sure did. He put the tray on the coffee table. I'm from Sydney." He pointed at his friends. "This is Jean-Luc from Biarritz and Dave from New Jersey."

"Hi," Megan said. "Hope you have a good day tomorrow."

"Should do," Dave said. "Great waves are forecast. Lots of surfers from all over the world, so the place will be hopping."

"I'll go and watch tomorrow," Megan promised. "Good luck."

The men smiled and nodded. Megan went upstairs and started to make up beds.

Beata joined her a little later. "Thanks for helping out."

Megan flicked a sheet open over the bed. "No problem. You'll have a busy weekend. Are you sure you don't need my room?"

Beata stuffed a pillow into a pillowcase. "No, yours is a small double. They want twin beds so they can share, and they need the bigger rooms. But I'm afraid I'm all booked out after the weekend. The summer will be very busy, right into August. But you were just staying until Sunday night anyway, weren't you?"

Megan sank down on the bed. "I was but… now that I'm here and have been to the house again, I'm beginning to feel I should stay around for a bit longer. I haven't much to go back to, really. I lost my job and have to move in with my mother."

Beata joined her on the bed. "Why don't you stay then? I could use some help, so if you'd like to earn a little bit of money, it might suit you, too."

Megan pondered this for a moment. "What sort of things would you want me to do?"

"Boris and I do the breakfasts, so that's okay. Then we have to make beds, clean rooms, do the shopping. You could help with that. Maybe be here in the afternoon when guests arrive to say welcome and give them a cup of tea. Organise the online bookings. I can pay you two hundred euros a week during the high season, as we have so many guests."

"Yes… well… that sounds fine. I wouldn't mind that at all. But—"

"Yes?"

"I have no place to stay."

"Yes, you do. You have a house only ten minutes' drive from here."

"But it's a wreck," Megan protested.

"So go camp in it. It's the summer. All you need is a roof over your head. I've some stuff left over from when this place was done up, all piled in the garage. I'm sure we can find a mattress at least."

"Oh, well…"

Beata pushed at Megan. "Go on, don't be a wimp. You have to decide what to do with it, one way or another. It's your house."

"Yes, I suppose you're right. But live in it?"

Beata gave her another shove. "Go and claim it before someone else grabs it."

"How do you mean?"

"That house is hot property, you know. A lot of people would kill to own it."

CHAPTER 6

"Hot property," Megan grunted, pulling her end of the mattress up creaking stairs. "That's a laugh."

"You just don't know anything about land or what sells," Beata panted at her end lower down. "Come on, stop moaning and get this bastard up."

Megan stopped to wipe sweat from her upper lip. "Why did Boris have to go and have a surf lesson just today? He could have thrown this up with his little finger."

Beata put the mattress down for a moment. "Boys have to have their fun. I have to let him out now and then, otherwise he gets morose. Drinks vodka and sings Russian songs about the Volga and bursts into tears. Letting him surf is easier."

Megan laughed. "You two have the strangest relationship."

Beata lifted the mattress. "Works for me. Come on, I haven't got all day."

They finally got the mattress up the stairs and into the front bedroom, where they propped it on its side. Megan opened the sash window. "At least this one isn't broken."

"You should get the broken ones fixed," Beata remarked. "I'm sure the frames need to be replaced, too but if you get someone to put in new glass it'll do for now."

"That's the first thing on my list. That and having the back door repaired." Megan took the brush Beata had lent her. The floorboards were covered in a thick layer of dust and mouse droppings. A stale smell rose as she brushed. She wrinkled her nose and tried to breathe through her mouth.

"You should wash the floor with hot water and a little bit of bleach," Beata suggested. "I put some stuff in the bucket I left downstairs."

"Where am I going to get hot water?" Megan stopped brushing. "Oh God, Beata, how am I going to live here in this wreck?"

Beata sighed. "Megan. Look at this house. It has great potential. The roof's okay, you have water. You probably need to rewire, and that might cost you a bit. Get an electrician to look it over and give you a quote. Why do I have to tell you all this?"

Megan looked thoughtfully at Beata. "You're right. I have to do this or not. No half measures."

Beata nodded. "That's right." She went to the window and leaned out. "The views are amazing from here. You're practically on the beach. I can hear the waves." She turned around and folded her arms. "This place is very valuable, you know."

"Yeah, right. It's a palace," Megan jeered.

Beata shook her head and rolled her eyes. "It's not about the house. Even though it's a sweet house that can be made to look really good. It's about the *location*. To farmers around here, fields with a stream are worth gold. Cattle don't have to be watered, and the growth is very good."

"Growth? What are you going on about?"

"You obviously know less about farming than I do. But stick around, and you'll hear farmers talk about 'the growth' all the time. It's either good or bad. Mostly bad. Anyway," she breezed on, "that's why farmers will be after the fields you have here. You could probably sell them off for a good whack and keep the house."

"I don't know if I want to do that," Megan said. "But go

on. I feel there's more wisdom coming."

Beata nodded. "Just this. The location of the house is great for tourism."

"Tourism," Megan said. "I thought that was dead."

"No, it's not dead, it's changing. The B-and-B business used to be about American tourists throwing their dollars around. But that was a long time ago. Before nine eleven and the economy landing in the toilet. The Yanks stay at home these days. And the car touring is not great because of petrol prices. But people now want adventure on holiday. Activities like walking, swimming, snorkelling. And here, on this side of Dingle, surfing is *king*. And kite surfing. And windsurfing. All year around." Beata drew breath.

Megan leaned on the brush handle, absorbing what Beata had just told her. "I see. Hmm, never thought of it that way."

"The fields could be sold in lots for building holiday cottages."

Megan wrinkled her nose. "I don't think I'd like that."

"I know, but keeping the fields as they are might be a luxury you can't afford."

"Hmm, I suppose. Lots to think about here."

"I know." Beata touched Megan's shoulder. "I have to get back. Can you come over and help me with the beds when you've finished?"

"Okay."

"Thanks." Beata bounded down the stairs. She stopped halfway. "I'll give the electricity board a call. Ask them to come and connect you."

"Brilliant. You're an angel."

"I wouldn't go that far," Beata laughed and slammed the front door.

There was an eerie silence when Beata had left, as if the house itself had listened to her words. Megan shook her head and got busy. Having swept the floor, she got water from the tap outside the back door and washed the floorboards with liquid soap mixed with a little bleach. The task done and the window frame given the same treatment as the floor, the room seemed instantly more inviting. A breeze from the sea lifted the threadbare curtains, and the sun shone on clean floorboards. A dove landed on the windowsill, cooing and cocking its head as if to study the room.

Megan left the mattress and went downstairs to inspect the kitchen and air out the rooms downstairs. Distant rumble from the fields opposite the house didn't register much at first. But as she opened the window in the front room, her nose was assaulted by a smell so foul it made her gasp. She staggered backwards. The smell was like a gas that invaded the house, drifted all around and permeated the very fabric of everything around her, even her clothes. She put her hand over her mouth and tried not to gag. What on earth was this…this *poison*?

* * *

"Slurry," Paudie said on the phone. "Jack must be spreading early."

"What? Who's Jack and why is he spreading this gas all over the place?"

"It's not gas, it's *slurry*, girl. Have you never heard of it?"

It dawned on Megan what he meant. "Oh shit!"

"Yup, that's it. Shit. Also known as slurry. Usually cow shit but Jack uses pig slurry, which is stronger."

"Oh. Is this allowed? What about the environment? I mean it's like a gas. Must be very polluting."

"We don't use that word much around here. Slurry's important for growth, you know. We all have to make a living."

"Yeah, but…" Megan swallowed. "How often does this

happen?"

"Depends."

"On what?"

"The weather. What crops need doing. How much there is in the cesspit. That sort of thing."

Megan groaned inwardly. "What can I do about this? I mean I can't have this smell around my house. It's disgusting."

Paudie laughed. "Do? Not much. But you have two options."

"Yes? What are they?"

"One, put up with it."

"And the other option?"

"Go back to Dublin."

* * *

"Light a fire," Beata said when they were carrying dirty sheets and towels downstairs.

"What do you mean?"

Beata threw the pile of laundry on the kitchen floor. "The fireplace. Light a fire and some candles. Close the windows. That should get rid of the smell indoors. And you know, Paudie is right. You have to get used to it. In any case it's so windy around here, the smell of slurry usually disappears in a day or so."

"Okay. I suppose you're right. Can't expect things to be the same as they are in the city."

Beata stuffed a pillowcase full of sheets. "I'll take this to the laundry tomorrow when I go shopping in Tralee. Let's have some tea."

Megan folded the towels and put them on the table. "Thanks, but I think I'll get back to the house. I want to light that fire and make up the bed and clean the bathroom. If you're sure there's nothing else you want me to do."

"No. The new guests are arriving soon, so I have to serve them tea, but I can manage. There's some wood in the shed you can have for your fire and half a bale of briquettes. I'll give you some firelighters and matches."

"Thank you. That'd be great."

Beata shrugged. "Least I can do when you've worked so hard. Can't tell you what a relief it is to have some help. I'll get Boris to put all that in the car for you." She opened the door to the hall. "Boris!" she yelled. "Get your arse in the kitchen."

Boris bounded in through the back door. "What you want? I was cleaning the van like you told me."

"Two fucking hours ago," Beata groaned. "Get a bag of wood and the briquettes from the shed, and put it into Megan's car, will you?"

"Yes, boss."

"Aren't you a little harsh with him?" Megan said when he had left.

Beata shrugged. "Maybe. But he's so lazy I have to whip him all the time."

Megan let out a laugh. "I bet you're also enjoying ordering a Russian around."

Beata smirked. "It's delicious. Like kicking the whole Russian army in the ass."

"Poor Boris."

"Ha, he likes it. Why else does he stick around?"

Megan picked up her bag. "Because he loves you?"

Beata's eyes hardened. "Don't say that again. Ever."

* * *

It was dusk by the time Megan returned to the house. She stopped for supper at a fish and chip shop on her way, bought candles, milk and bread and then took a detour to look at the sunset over Brandon Bay.

The house was dark. Except for a lingering odour, the smell had abated. Megan lugged in the bag of firewood and put her shopping on the kitchen table. She went out and picked some of the daisies and wild roses and put them in a jar. The kitchen tap was stiff, but she finally managed to turn it. Seconds later she wished she hadn't, as water shot out of the tap. It soaked her shirt and jeans in an instant. Gasping, she tried to turn off the tap, but it came off in her hand, the water still gushing and soaking the floor.

In a panic she ran to her phone. She hesitated. Who to call? What to do? The water still shot out of the tap with enormous pressure. She had to get it to stop. Oh, yes, of course. In a flash of inspiration, she knew who to call.

* * *

"There," Paudie said, walking back from the gate. "I shut off the water."

"Thank God you were home," Megan sighed, pulling her wet shirt away from her body. "And thank God you had that key to turn off the stopcock."

"You probably have one lying around somewhere too."

"Ha, I wouldn't know how to use it if I had one. Thanks for coming. Sorry if I disturbed you. But you did say I could call if there was anything."

Paudie put the stopcock key into his jeep. "No problem, girl. Sorry you had this trouble."

Megan leaned on the gate. "I have to get that tap replaced, I suppose."

Paudie laughed. "The tap? That's not all, darlin'. You need to redo the whole plumbing. The pipes are made of lead. Haven't been seen to since the dawn of creation."

"Nooo," Megan moaned. "How much will that cost? And the rewiring on top of that?"

Paudie shrugged. "Cost? Dunno. An arm and a leg and the shirt off your back and a little extra change."

"Shit." Megan kicked the gate.

"That's old houses for you. They eat money." Paudie got into the jeep. "But of course, you have the stream. Plenty of water there. Got to go. See you around, Megs."

He drove off in a shower of gravel and mud.

* * *

Exhausted and downcast, Megan went back inside and mopped up the water on the kitchen floor with old rags she found in the shed. Feeling cold, she changed her shirt and jeans and hung up her wet things in the bathroom. She decided to go downstairs to light that fire. She stacked kindling, logs and a firelighter in the grate and stuck the candles in two jam jars she found in the kitchen. Then she set a match to the pile in the grate. Bright flames soon flickered around the logs, which, with the candlelight, made the room instantly more inviting.

Megan sat on the padded seat and looked at the fire, feeling for the first time she was home. The feeling didn't last long. Once the fire had taken, the smoke didn't rise into the chimney anymore, but began to fill the room.

What was the problem? Megan peered through the smoke up the chimney and saw nothing but a mass of twigs. Crows. They must have blocked the chimney trying to nest. "Why didn't I think of that," Megan sobbed as she tried to put out the fire with an old blanket. But the blanket caught fire and the smell of burning wool made everything worse. She finally filled one of the jam jars with water from the stream and threw it on the smouldering mess and went back out for more. Several trips later, the fire finally turned into a black pile, emitting an acrid stench.

Gasping for air, her eyes streaming, Megan stumbled outside and collapsed on the back step. She put her head on her arms and gave herself up to frustration and despair. The tears came slowly at first, welling up from deep inside, her sense of failure with the fire adding to all the pent-up emotions she had suppressed for months, years even.

Her father's death. Stephen's betrayal. Losing her job. The house and the problems it presented. A desperate sense of loneliness. It all mingled into one big, unbearable pain. Her sobs echoed into the stillness of the summer night, drowning the sound of the stream and even the waves crashing onto the beach.

A hand on her shoulder. She screamed.

"Stop screaming. It's me."

She turned around and peered at the face, barely visible in the gloom. "Dan?" she whispered. "What are you doing here?"

"I came to give you something. But never mind." He joined her on the step and put his arm around her. "What's the matter?"

Megan sighed and snivelled. She wiped her nose with the back of her hand. "I'm all snotty."

"Here." He handed her a handkerchief. "It's clean. Blow your nose. Wipe your tears, and tell Uncle Dan why you're sitting here crying your eyes out."

Megan dried her face and blew her nose. "Thanks." She sighed.

"That sigh came from somewhere very deep," Dan remarked.

"Yes."

"Want to talk about it?"

"No."

"Okay."

She leaned against him. "You smell of the sea."

He put his nose in her hair. "You stink of smoke."

"I know. I lit a fire to get rid of the smell of slurry, but I was stupid enough not to have checked the chimney first so—" She started to cry again. "I'm so useless. I can't even light a fire. And this place smells of shit, and I can't even get up enough energy to make my bed. And the plumbing is crap and needs to be replaced. And I must get the house rewired. God knows what else. It's going to cost a fortune. The farmers hate me, and I have nowhere else to go."

He wrapped his arms around her in a tight hug. "There," he murmured, "go on, cry. Let it all out."

"I'll have to sell the house," Megan wept into his shirt. "I love it so much, and I wanted to stay here, but now I can't."

He hugged her tighter. "That's awful. But maybe for the best. An old house like this is a lot for a woman to cope with. For anyone, come to think of it."

"It sure is." Megan pulled back and wiped her face. "It's okay. I feel better now. Thanks."

"Sure?"

"Yes. Everything just felt so hopeless. Sorry about this. Must pull myself together." But she didn't want to lose the warmth and comfort of his arms. She snuggled closer. *I don't know him. I have only met him twice. He's smug and superior. But why do I suddenly feel so attracted to him? Why does it feel so good to be in his arms, even though he's only trying to be nice?* She looked into his face, trying to see the look in his eyes. But it was too dark.

"Megan," he whispered, his mouth on her cheek. "You're so sweet and so sad." His mouth found hers.

She pulled back, but gave up the struggle. Their lips met in a long kiss. *What am I doing? Who cares*, she answered back, *it's fabulous.* His lips were warm, his breath sweet. He smelled faintly of the sea and some kind of spicy aftershave. But something at the back of her mind made her pull away.

"Please… Dan… I can't."

"Why not?" He pulled her close again and kissed her mouth.

She relaxed for a moment and let herself go, then pushed him away again. "Dan, please. Stop."

They pulled apart, panting.

"I'm sorry," she mumbled.

"No, I should apologise. Don't know what happened. I don't usually take advantage of women in this way. But you were sitting there, so sweet and soft and sad."

"I'm a mess," Megan mumbled and touched her hair.

"You're beautiful. When you walked into the pub on Saturday night, everybody was looking at you."

"Yeah," Megan said with a snort. "Probably because I stuck out like a tart at a funeral."

"Shut up." He tried to kiss her again.

She pulled back. "Please. I can't. Not now."

Dan touched her face and ran his hand down her neck, then lightly touched her breasts. "Sweet girl," he whispered.

She shivered and caught his hand. "It's too soon."

"I know." He squeezed her hand. "But we can work on it."

"Maybe." She pulled away and cleared her throat. "So, why did you come here? What was it you wanted to give me?"

He got up. "Oh, uh… I had this box of stuff. Your Uncle Pat's belongings. The nursing home gave it to me. Not much in it. His watch. Some photos and letters and little knick-knacks he had in his room there. But I thought you should have it."

"Thanks."

"I put it on the kitchen table."

She looked up at him. "I'll go and do up my bed now. I feel like sleeping forever."

Dan hovered on the path. "Are you sure you can manage?"

She got to her feet. "Yes. I'm fine."

"Sure?"

"Absolutely."

He put his hand on her shoulder. "Can I call you?"

"Yes." She couldn't think of what else to say.

"See you soon." With that, he padded around the side of the house and disappeared.

Megan listened to his car drive off, with a feeling her life had just taken a very strange turn.

CHAPTER 7

"This needs updating. And the kitchen too."

Megan opened her eyes. Bright sunlight blinded her for a moment. Confused, she looked around the room. Then she remembered. She was in her house, on a mattress in the front bedroom. That voice? Must have been the tail end of a dream. She stretched and yawned, feeling rested for the first time in weeks.

The voice spoke again: a male voice. "Great views even from the bathroom. And the land stretches nearly all the way to the beach. We could get at least twenty mobile homes into the fields there."

"Yes, but the house is in a bad state," a woman's voice said. "Maybe it would be better to just knock it down? You could put up a nice little bungalow here."

Megan tore out of her improvised bed. She threw on a shirt, opened the door and stared at the couple on the landing, who stared back at her as if she were a ghost. "Who are you?" Megan demanded. "What are you doing here?"

"Who are *you*?" the man demanded. "Are you squatting here?"

The woman crept behind her companion. "We're looking at the house. It's for sale."

"What?" Megan wrapped the shirt tighter around her. "For sale? Says who?"

"This website." The man waved a piece of paper at Megan. "Kerry farmhouse near beach and mountains. In need of some repairs," he said with a sneer. "That's the understatement of the year." He spoke with a cut-glass British accent.

Megan blinked. "What website?" She snatched the paper from the man. "What's this? Daft.ie... Oh. It's on the web. I had no idea." She shrugged and smiled. "I'm sorry. I'm the new owner. My uncle left me the property in his will. I had no idea it was still up on the Internet."

The man looked sternly at her. "Can you prove it?"

"Prove what?" Megan asked.

"That you're the owner. Do you have deeds or any other proof of ownership?"

Megan took a step back. "Yes...I mean, no. It's with some of the things I left in the B and B I stayed in last night."

"In that case, we can still look around." The man took the piece of paper from Megan.

Megan felt a rising irritation. "Who gave you keys to get in, if you don't mind my asking?"

"Uh," the woman piped up, "we don't have keys. We found this on the Internet and thought we'd come to have a look. The back door was open, so—"

"You thought it was okay to break in?"

"We didn't break in," the man said. "The door was open."

"It's broken," Megan snapped. "But in any case, wouldn't it have been more correct to call the estate agent and make an appointment for a viewing?" She marched into her room and found her phone. "I'm calling my solicitor. He can confirm what I just said."

The woman tugged at the man's sleeve. "Alistair. Please. Let's go. We can check this out with the estate agent."

The man didn't move. He kept looking at Megan, as if he was torn between believing her or brazing it out. "All right.

We'll leave." He dug into the inside pocket of his wax jacket. "Here's my card. If you really are the owner and you'd be interested in selling, give me a call."

"I'd prefer you to contact the agent, and make an offer." Megan took the card. "Then I can consider it and maybe negotiate a price."

"Very well. We'd like to look into buying the whole property with the land," The man said in a more polite tone. "It has planning permission for a caravan park. But we were thinking more like a boutique site. Very few mobile homes and a little fish restaurant."

"Sounds like a total nightmare," Megan said. "But we'll see. I'd like you to leave now, if you don't mind."

The woman started down the stairs. "Come on, Alistair. Can't you see we're disturbing her?"

Alistair followed her. "I'd be prepared to make a good offer," he said over his shoulder. "How about giving me a call when you've thought it over?"

"Talk to the agent, and I'll consider your offer," Megan said.

The door slammed. Megan padded to the window and watched them get into a Land Rover and drive off. She looked at the card. Alistair Cooper-Maxwell. An address in Weybridge, London. She stuffed it into the breast pocket of her shirt, leaned her elbows on the windowsill and looked at the beach, the blue ocean and the endless sky. She turned her face to the sun and closed her eyes, cleared her mind of what had just happened, and smiled as she thought of the kiss on the back step the night before.

* * *

"Why is my house advertised for sale on the Internet?" Megan tried to keep her voice cool.

"Is it? I had no idea." Dan's voice brought her instantly back to the night before. "How are you today?"

Megan cleared her suddenly dry throat. "I'm fine. Please answer the question. Oh, and another one. Is there planning permission for a caravan park?"

Dan paused. "Oh, yes. I remember now. That was an old thing. Pat applied for that about two years ago. But I think it's expired by now. Planning permissions last two years, and then you have to apply for a new one. I'll look up the date."

"I see." Megan put her hand to her chest, trying to slow down her heartbeat. "It's just that there was a couple here this morning, walking around the house, with details from Daft. ie. An English couple. I think he's some kind of developer. They just walked in. I was still in bed."

"Oh shit. I hope they didn't scare you."

"I got a bit of a fright, to tell you the truth. Of course, it was easy to just walk in. The lock is broken, and the hinges are so rusty on the door that it can't be closed properly. I've called a locksmith to come and fit a new lock later today. Don't want to be surprised like that again so early in the morning."

"Sorry about that. I'll get on to my dad. Tell him you want to sell."

"Okay." Megan paused. "Thanks."

"I'd like to see you again," Dan said after a brief silence. "Can I call around tonight?"

Her knees shaking, Megan sat down on one of Beata's kitchen chairs. "No," she heard herself say. "I… Could we meet at the pub?" She suddenly didn't want to be alone with him.

"Cold feet?" he asked with a hint of laughter.

"Mm. Something like that."

He laughed. "Okay. We'll go back to the beginning. A first date."

"That would be nice."

"Mulligans at seven? We can have dinner there."

"Great. I'm sure the door will be fixed by then. But I'll call you if there's a delay."

"Okay. See you then."

Megan hung up. She knew she should get the tea tray ready for guests arriving soon, but she couldn't move.

Beata, carrying two shopping bags, pushed the back door open. "Who was that?"

Megan smiled. "Hmm, yes ..." As if awakened from a deep sleep, she looked at Beata. "What?"

Beata put the shopping bags on the table. "I asked who were you talking to."

Megan came back to reality. "Dan Nolan."

"Oh. Did he explain why your house was still out there on the Internet? And if the planning permission thing was true?"

"Yes."

Beata leaned forward and stared at Megan's face. "Hello? Anybody home? What's wrong with you?"

Megan played with the fringe of the table cloth. "Nothing. Everything. He asked me out."

Beata sat down. "What? Dan Nolan asked you out? Why is this a problem?"

Megan looked at Beata. "I'm scared."

"Aha! Scared. Means you're hot for him, yes? And that you feel if you get involved, he'll hurt you in the end because of what that creepy husband did to you. And you don't want to go all the way because sex with the hubby was so fantastic, you don't think anyone can match that." She drew breath. "Or... you're afraid Danny boy *will* be an even better lay so, then you'll be twice as hurt."

Megan laughed. "You must be psychic." She sighed. "Yes, I'm scared. Not because of what he'll do but because I might mess it up again. The break-up of my marriage was partly my fault. I think I was too critical and demanding. And maybe I should have given him more support when he started that new job."

"Don't beat yourself up over it," Beata soothed. "Even if you were too demanding or whatever, couldn't it have been solved if you had talked about it?"

Megan sighed. "I don't know. Maybe. Stephen never wanted to discuss his feelings or mine. He didn't like conflicts. But maybe he really didn't want things to be resolved? Maybe he was happy to have an excuse to leave me?"

"No use crying over that now," Beata remarked. "This time you might be lucky. Or Dan might be the kind of guy who shares his feelings. But there's only one way to find out. And that's to go out with him and try to get to know him better."

"Probably," Megan agreed. "I'm not sure what I want to do."

"Do you know what I think you should do?" Beata sprang up from the table. "First, a shot of vodka. Then a cup of coffee. Then we'll get to work and serve tea to Mr and Mrs Lindholm from Sweden, who'll be arriving in about half an hour." She took a bottle and two shot glasses from a cupboard. "Then you're going to tart yourself up and look absolutely ring-a-ding-drop-dead gorgeous and knock Danny boy's eyes out. Sounds good so far?"

Megan giggled. "Yes, apart from the last bit. Don't think that will be possible."

Beata pushed a glass at Megan. "Here. Down the hatch. Gives you the courage of ten lions." She knocked back her own drink. "Ahhh. Great. Polish vodka. The best."

Megan picked up the glass. She looked at Beata and knocked back the drink. It hit her mouth like acid, then slid down her throat like a burning flame and settled in her stomach with a warm glow that instantly relaxed her. She smiled. "Wow. Yes. Thanks."

Beata waggled her finger at Megan. "You're going on that date. You're going to look fantastic. And you're going to have fun. That's an order."

"Yes, boss."

"And park all your feelings and fears at the door. If you just remember that all men are bastards who will break your heart in the end, you'll be all right." Beata started to make coffee.

"How do you manage that?"

Beata whipped around. "After that time with Paudie, I decided to act like a man. Take the sex, enjoy it but treat them like shit. Never, ever let them know how you feel about them. That keeps them guessing and scared."

Still feeling the afterglow, Megan put her glass on the table. "Scared? Because they don't know if you love them or not? If you'll dump them in the end?"

"You got it."

* * *

Beata's words rang through Megan's mind as she got ready to meet Dan. The bathroom in the old house was less than inviting, but the water from the stream she had hauled up in a bucket was soft on her skin and felt good despite the cold. She could have had a shower in Beata's bathroom but felt she needed to be alone before she faced Dan. She didn't want Beata to comment on her choice of white trousers and light blue shirt. Not sexy, but fresh and cool.

She inspected herself in the cracked mirror and was pleasantly surprised. She didn't look bad at all. Her red hair, washed in rainwater, shone with honey highlights. She had a light tan already and didn't need much make-up, apart from a touch of mascara.

Excitement made her cheeks pink. Fear gave her eyes a wide, vulnerable look she couldn't disguise. Treat them like shit, she said to herself as she grabbed her bag. This will be my new mantra.

* * *

She forgot the mantra when she spotted Dan at the bar. He looked as clean and fresh as she felt, in navy polo shirt and jeans, with his white sweater across his shoulders.

He rose as she approached, took her hand and kissed it. "Hello, gorgeous."

She pulled her hand away. "Hi."

He put his hands up. "Okay, first date. Won't put a finger on you all evening. Promise."

Disarmed, she smiled. "Good. I'll hold you to that."

"Door all fixed?"

"Yes. And the guy helped me fix the hinges, and he rehung the door as well. Wasn't cheap but worth it." She dug around in her handbag. "I have an extra set of keys here. Maybe you should have them in case something happens."

He pocketed the keys. "Okay. Good idea." He pulled out a chair. "But let's sit down and order a drink."

As they sat down, he said, "I have some news. An English businessman has made an offer on your house. A bit more than the original bid. Two hundred and seventy K, he said. But he wants to do a survey before he buys."

"Really? Must be the guy who barged in when I was asleep." Megan paused. "I'll think about it. Sounds like a good offer, though."

"It is. But let's not talk business on our first date."

Megan returned his wide smile. "Yes. First date. Feels a little silly to be on a date at my age, but what else is it?"

"Well, whatever it is, we'll take it nice and slow. I can tell that's what you want."

"Your powers of observation are right this time."

He laughed. "Yes, I think they're back. And I actually like taking it slowly. Go with the flow, you know?"

* * *

He kept his word. Awkward at first, a glass of wine helped to make her feel a little more relaxed. They chatted casually over dinner. Dan was courteous and pleasant. Megan began to think she had dreamed the kiss on the back step. And maybe she had. She returned his gaze with cool detachment, while repeating Beata's mantra over and over in her mind.

"Coffee?" Dan asked.

Megan jumped. "What? Sorry. I was miles away."

"Am I boring you?"

"No. It's been fun. But I have so much to think about. These past few days have been incredibly busy. I feel as if I've stepped into some kind of other dimension, or a parallel universe. Mad, isn't it?"

He laughed. "No, it's just Kerry. It's like another planet."

"The dark side of the moon, my mother says. But she doesn't like Kerry much."

He raised his eyebrows. "Why?"

Megan ran her finger around the rim of her glass. "I don't really know. I think there was some kind of row when we were here that summer. I remember the last few days. My mother was very quiet, and Uncle Pat and Aunt Molly didn't talk much to either of my parents. Then we never went back."

"The letters I brought you might throw some light on it." Dan waved to a waitress. "Did you say yes to coffee?"

She shook her head. "No. Can't drink coffee this late, or

I won't sleep."

"Doesn't bother me. I'll have a coffee, please," he said to the waitress. He turned back to Megan. "You haven't told me much about yourself."

She laughed. "Probably because we were busy talking about you."

"Well, you asked. A lot. And I replied."

"A lot."

"Uh, yes." He looked at her with curiosity. "So who are you, Megan O'Farrell? Tell me."

She shrugged. "Nothing much to tell. I'm quite ordinary really. At a loose end right now, I suppose. I lost my job at the department store. Seem to have lost my husband too."

"I'm sorry. I didn't know you were a widow."

"No," Megan said. "We broke up."

"Oh." Dan looked relieved. "I thought he was dead."

Megan shrugged. "He is to me. I've killed him a thousand times in my imagination. A slow, painful death, involving private parts. Very comforting and healing."

He laughed.

She glared at him. "You think that's funny? My husband left me. That didn't make me laugh. Oh, I know, it's a classic. Husband falls for younger, more attractive woman. Hilarious."

He put a hand on her arm. "No, I didn't mean—"

She pulled away. "I know what you're thinking. But do you want to know what *I'm* thinking right now?"

He looked uncertain. "Yes? No… maybe I don't. I have a feeling a barrage is coming, and I don't have anywhere to hide."

She stood up, the chair scraping on the floor like nails on a blackboard. "I'm thinking, if you really want to know, that here I am, at the age of thirty-eight on a fecking *date*. Like a teenager. And you're sitting there, thinking I'm easy meat."

He shot to his feet. "I didn't think—"

"Yes, you did. You all do." She held out her hand. "Let's go back to where we were. Client and solicitor."

He took her hand and held it in both of his. "Please, Megan. Sit down. Don't leave in a huff."

His beguiling smile melted her anger. Feeling foolish, Megan sighed and smiled. "I was going to leave in my car, actually." She pulled away her hand and sat down. "You're right. I overreacted. Sorry. I'm still a bit raw."

He settled back on his chair. "It's quite understandable. And I'm really sorry about all of that. Can't have been easy."

"No. But I shouldn't take it out on you." She smiled at him. "I'm really sorry about that."

He put his hand on hers. "That's absolutely okay. I understand how strange it must feel to be out on a date or whatever you want to call it."

Megan breathed a sigh of relief. "Thank you. I really appreciate you being so understanding. These past few days have been a bit confusing too, with the house and everything."

He withdrew his hand. "Of course. So, on the subject of the house… You want to sell, is that it? Must say, I'm not surprised."

Megan sighed. "I don't have a choice. The repairs are going to cost too much. I do have some money after the sale of our house in Dublin, but I'm afraid to spend it all on this house. Even with my severance pay and the salary Beata pays me, I still have to sign on the dole to get that little bit of extra. It would be crazy to sink all my savings into a house."

Dan nodded. "Yes, I see that. You should sell. That offer I told you about is a good one. You should take it. Then you could of course buy a small place around here, as you like the area so much. Or a mobile home out on the Maharees."

"True. I could. Won't be the same, though. The location of Uncle Pat's house is unique. I haven't seen anything like it in this area."

Dan nodded at the waitress as she arrived with the coffee. "Thanks." He turned to Megan. "You could sell the land and stay in the house. But then you'll probably have a caravan park next door."

"Not something I'd like to live with," Megan agreed.

They were interrupted by the sound of a tin whistle playing a slow, lilting tune. A woman's voice joined in, singing a lament in Gaelic.

"Forgot to tell you," Dan whispered. "It's music night. Traditional music every Tuesday evening here. You don't mind?"

Megan shook her head. "No. It's lovely."

They listened in silence to the song, replaced by a livelier tune when two more musicians arrived, playing banjo and fiddle. More guests piled in, until the pub was so crowded, there was no place to sit down.

Forgetting all her problems, the music transported Megan to happier times. The rhythm and harmony of the instruments and sweet lilt of the voices lifted her mood and stirred her senses. She moved to sit beside Dan. He put his arm around her with an apologetic little smile. She shrugged and smiled back, enjoying the close comfort.

The music stopped for a brief intermission. Dan pulled Megan up. "Let's go outside. It's getting a little too hot in here."

They bumped into Beata in the doorway, on her way back in after a cigarette.

"Hi there," Megan said.

Beata studied them for a moment. "Hi there. Leaving already? I just arrived."

"We've been here since early this evening," Dan said. "So now we're coming out for some air."

Beata looked at their entwined hands. "Ooooh. I seeeee."

Megan blushed. "No. It's—"

"None of your business," Dan said and pulled Megan with him out the door. "You should quit smoking. Gives you wrinkles and black teeth."

"Fuck off."

"We will," Dan said over his shoulder. "Charming girl," he muttered in Megan's ear.

They walked to the edge of the beach overlooking Brandon bay. The sun slowly sank into the ocean. The mountains, in hues of blue and purple, sloped down to the azure water. The air was still, the sea like glass.

Megan leaned on the wall. Lost in the spectacular beauty of the summer evening, she forgot about Dan and Beata and let her mind go. An odd feeling came over her. Like balloons carried by a soft breeze, her sorrows and concerns drifted away into space. She felt a lightness of being, the parting of a pain that had been gnawing at her for a long time. Suddenly, her spirits soared, and she knew, with strange clarity, that someone or something had given her the strength to carry on.

She turned to Dan. "Thank you."

As if noticing a change in her, he took a step away. "For what?"

"For this evening." She made a sweeping gesture with her hand. "For this."

He laughed. "I didn't make the mountains. Or the ocean."

"No, but you brought me here tonight. There's something special—" She breathed out, unable to go on. He would probably think she was mad.

He put his arm around her shoulders. "I know."

They watched the sun disappear into the ocean.

Dan shivered and laughed. "It's getting a little chilly." He pulled her closer. "Do you want to—?"

She pulled away. "No. I have to go."

"Where?" he asked.

"Home."

CHAPTER 8

After arriving back at the house, Megan walked around the garden in the dusk. At the bank of the stream, she sat down on a tree stump. The soothing sound of the water calmed her, and the breeze gently lifting her hair was like a caress. She looked up and spotted a lone star in the darkening sky. She breathed in the soft air and closed her eyes for a moment. *Should I really leave? Give up and go back to Dublin? Sell the house to the highest bidder?* She looked at the dark shape of the house. *So much to do and I haven't even started yet.* The windows were like black eyes, staring at her, waiting for a decision. The door slowly swung open in a sudden gust of wind. Megan knew she had forgotten to lock it, but it looked as if the house beckoned her to go in, like a mother telling her child it was time for bed.

Once inside, she picked up the box with Uncle Pat's belongings and took it with her upstairs. Settled into bed, she lit a candle and opened the box. She took out a wad of letters and flicked through them. Nothing much. Some old bills, bank statements, signed agreements for the conacre contract, which were renewed each year. Christmas cards. Letters of condolence on the death of Auntie Molly.

She delved deeper and fished out some postcards and newspapers clippings. An old silver watch on a chain. She held it in her hand and touched the smooth surface. A beautiful little thing.

Rummaging further in the box, her fingers found something square and hard. A small, scuffed leather-bound book. Megan opened it. *Molly's book*, it said on the flyleaf. She turned the pages. A diary. But there were no dates, just entries with thoughts and prayers and the odd poem. Aunt Molly had simply jotted down her musings now and then. Maybe to fix things she liked in her mind so she wouldn't forget them?

Megan turned the first page.

I like planting bulbs. Because I know the flowers will come up every spring for many years to come, even after I'm long gone. It will be as if I'm saying hello to whomever is there, to whomever lives in my house, even fifty or a hundred years from now. This way I will leave a piece of me in this earth.

Megan smiled. What a lovely thought. I'll remember that when the daffodils come up in the spring. She seems such a happy woman. Maybe it's her loving presence I can feel in this house?

Summer. The lovely long evenings. Watching the swallows swoop and soar in the bright sky. Walking on the beach. Looking at the ships and wondering where they are going. Summer is both a joyful and sad season. I have my sadness, but God is good and has given me much to be happy about.

Megan wondered what sadness this could have been. The lack of children? Unhappy marriage? There was a melancholy to the little musings. Maybe life was harsh here in the old days? Maybe Molly was a woman who needed more than the simple routines of everyday life on a small farm?

Then a poem by W.B Yeats.

> *We rode in sorrow, with strong hounds three,*
> *Bran, Sgeolan, and Lomair,*
> *On a morning misty and mild and fair.*

The mist-drops hung on the fragrant trees,
And in the blossoms hung the bees.
We rode in sadness above Lough Lean,
For our best were dead on Gavra's green.

And Megan's own favourite, *Tread Softly*. She read the last line out loud. "Tread softly because you tread on my dreams."

She turned the page. What she read next made her sit up in bed. What did this mean? She read it again.

My husband's child. Not mine and never will be. I can't have any of my own but I don't want hers. A child by another woman, now dead. A child born outside marriage. I can't have him here. He'll have to go, I said. So it was decided. Little Sean will be brought up by Pat's brother, Rory. He will be better off there, on that big farm. Rory will make sure he gets a good education. Am I cruel? No. It would be cruel to keep him. He'll never know. But he'll never get the house or the land. That will go to my sister's children. I'll make sure of that.

* * *

"Mam, I need to know something."

"Megan? How are you? How's the house? Have you sold it yet?"

Megan sat down on the windowsill in her bedroom. "No. Look, there's something I need to ask you. Something important."

"What? Megan, if there's something wrong, you should come home. Stop this nonsense and look for a job."

"I have a job."

"A job? Doing what?"

Megan sighed. "Working in a B and B."

"In a B and B? Like a waitress? With your qualifications,

that's all you could find?"

"It's just a temporary thing. But never mind. Will you listen for a minute, Mam?"

"All right. I'm listening."

Megan cleared her suddenly dry throat. "It's about Dad. I need to know... about his parents."

"Yes?" Her mother's voice was suddenly faint.

"Was Uncle Pat his real father?"

Silence.

"Mam? Are you there?"

"Yes."

"So?"

She could hear her mother breathing at the other end. Then, "How did you find out?"

"So it's true then?"

"Yes. Oh, Megan, we didn't want to tell anyone. Very few people knew. And they're all dead anyway. We found out about it that summer in Kerry, when you were eight."

Megan pressed the phone closer to her ear. "Is that why Dad was so upset? Why we never went back?"

"Yes, Megan. That's why. He couldn't forgive Pat for not telling the truth. And for giving him away to his brother. He didn't have a very happy childhood, you see." Her mother sighed. "Oh, it's all so complicated and sad. Nothing to do with you."

"I know. But it would have been good to know. To understand why Dad was the way he was." A thought struck Megan. "What about his real mother? Who was she?"

"Nobody knew. She died when your dad was only two. Then he was brought to Pat. Molly wouldn't have anything to do with him. Everybody is *dead*, Megan. Don't start digging up graves. Haven't we had enough sadness?"

Megan felt tears well up. "Yes. You're right. But it's good to know. Of course, this is the reason Pat willed me his house."

"Yes. Of course."

"Molly wanted it to go to her family."

"Probably. But that's not your problem now. You'll get a lot of money for that house and the bit of land."

"I would. If I were selling it."

* * *

Megan didn't get much time to think or do much about her house during the following weeks. The fully booked B and B meant a lot of work. Beata was a fair but tough boss and kept Megan to her agreed hours without as much as a coffee break. But as Beata worked as hard herself, Megan couldn't complain. She enjoyed the buzz of the comings and goings of visitors from all over the world, loved showing them the maps of the area and pointing out places of beauty and interest, developing a pride in a part of the world she began to think of as hers.

The electrician arrived. He gave her a quote that sounded exorbitant, but Beata just nodded and said it was what she would have expected. Megan accepted the quote, and it only took a few days to do the job and get connected. She gritted her teeth and paid the bill.

The plumbing was a different matter. The plumber, recommended by Paudie, walked around the house, scratching his head and muttering to himself while he made a list. "All the pipes will have to be replaced. A new immersion tank. New taps and a new shower. Replacing the septic tank, but that's a job for a specialist firm."

"Yes?" Megan said. "And how much will that cost?"

He shook his head. "Don't know. Could be around five thousand euros or so. You'll have to get a firm to come and take a look. But I could do something temporary with the old system until you can get it changed."

"Oh, good."

"Then you need an immersion for the hot water and a tank up in the attic. There must have been some kind of solid fuel cooker here once with a back boiler."

Megan nodded. "Yes, there was. It's been removed though."

"Which is a good thing. It was probably not working very well."

"No," Megan agreed. "So, how much would you say your work will cost?"

He paused and looked at his list. "Hard to say. I have to do my sums and then see what the material will come to."

Megan groaned. "I understand all that, but how about a wild guess? You know, a ballpark figure?"

"Hmm, yes…" He studied his list. "Well, let's say around seven."

"Seven—what?"

"Grand."

"What?" Megan shrieked. "Seven thousand euros?"

He nodded "Yup, roundabout that."

"Oh God."

"Yeah, well…" He stuck his biro behind his ear. "Okay, I might be able to squeeze it down to six and half."

"Oh, gee. Thanks," Megan sighed.

The plumber looked around the kitchen. "These old houses are expensive to do up. You'll probably need a new kitchen. And I couldn't help noticing that the whole house needs a good paint job inside and out and new gutters too. I'd sell the lot if I were you."

"So would I," Megan sighed. "If I wasn't mad enough to love it."

He looked at her with pity. "That kind of love leads to bankruptcy in the end."

"I know. When can you start?"

"Next week."

* * *

"Why are you doing this?" Dan said when he phoned to ask her out. "I thought you said you were selling? You said—"

Megan sighed and sat down on the sofa in Beata's living room. "I know what I said. But that was before—"

"Before what? Before you knew Pat was your real grandfather?"

"Yes." Megan lowered her voice and glanced into the deserted hall. "Please, Dan, don't tell anyone about that. I want to keep it quiet. Don't want those awful Quinn brothers to find out."

"Okay, won't tell a soul. But, sweetheart, it's crazy to spend all this money to do the house up. Why don't you consider what I said? Sell it and buy a smaller place. Or at least sell the land."

"No!" Megan stood up. "Don't ever say that again. Sell the land? It's *mine*. It belongs to my family. It's in my *blood*."

Dan sighed and laughed. "Such passion. Wish you were that hot for me."

"I am… I mean… I might be. Soon." Megan knew what he meant. She had been holding back, trying not to get too close. If she did, she might get hurt, might get left again like the last time. Their kisses were hot, his sweet words so seductive and his body… Nearly aroused just thinking about being in his arms, feeling his hands on her skin, she pushed the thoughts away. "I'm sorry about that last time, Dan. But I explained."

"I know." He paused. "Maybe we should take a break? Not see each other for a while? Give you space and time to think?"

Megan hesitated. It wasn't fair to behave like a teenager with him, letting it get so far each time and then pulling away. She had to make a decision. She hadn't had sex in over a year. She needed it, wanted it. She felt warm all over when she thought of Dan. Why was this such a problem? "I—" she started. "No, I don't want to take a break. I want… to get closer to you."

He was silent for so long she thought he had hung up. Then he coughed. "Oh? That sounds like good news. So… how about tonight? You're free?"

"Yes," she whispered.

"I'll pick you up at seven."

"Where are we going?"

He laughed. "To somewhere very nice, I hope."

Megan hung up with a feeling she had crossed some kind of Rubicon.

"Problems?" Beata walked in with a pile of logs for the fire.

"No. Yes. Dan."

Beata piled the logs into the fireplace. "Not that again." She turned around. "Please, Megan, It's boring. Sleep with him if you want. Or don't. Your problem, not mine. Just don't ask what I think you should do a hundred times a day. You don't listen to what I say, anyway."

"I won't mention it again. I'm seeing him tonight. Have no idea what's going to happen."

Beata winked. "Hot sex, I hope. Now, concentrate on the house. I don't understand why you're spending every cent you have on it."

"Because it belongs to my family. Always has, Paudie said. The O'Farrells have been there since the beginning of time. That ruined tower on my land was built by my ancestors in the fifteenth century. My great-great grandfather cleared all the stones and rocks out of the land and grew things on it. Had his little farm on it and fed his family and all the families after that. How can I sell it? It wouldn't be right."

Beata nodded. "Just like in that movie I saw on TV last night. *The Field*. Must be something Irish. This thing about land."

"Yes, I think it is."

"More important than sex?"

"Much more."

* * *

In her underwear, Megan caught her reflection in the bedroom window. The shape she saw was round and feminine. The bra pushed her breasts into a very pleasing cleavage, making her waist look smaller. Her wide hips and firm thighs completed the picture of a mature, shapely woman. Normally so critical of her unfashionable shape, Megan now felt proud of her body. This is me, she thought, take it or leave it, Dan Nolan.

He did. His eyes on her when she got into the car were appreciative, to say the least. His hand on her shoulders, and his light kiss sent hot sparks into her groin. "Where are you taking me?" she asked with intended innuendo.

He winked. "I haven't quite decided where yet. But we'll eat first."

"Where? Mulligans?"

"No. Better than that." He started the car. "We're going out to the Maharees. A pal of mine has a cottage there. He's away, so he lent it to me for the weekend."

"Perfect," Megan purred.

He shot her an amused glance. "For what?"

She smiled innocently. "Well, you know. For watching the sunset." She stretched, arching her back. "Oh, I'm so stiff. My back is killing me. Working for Beata is no holiday."

He glanced at her breasts. "I'll give you a massage when I get the chance."

She closed her eyes and smiled. "That would be wonderful."

He laughed. "Enough of this, or I might just throw you

on the lawn and ravish you. But being a gentleman, I want to wine and dine you first."

"Sounds wonderful. I could do with a little wining and dining."

The cottage was at the end of the little peninsula. Overlooking the harbour, it had spectacular views of the sea. The sun was still warm, the wind balmy. With the sound of the waves and the distant cry of seagulls, there was a wonderful peace there. A feeling of being at the end of a continent.

Megan gazed at the horizon. "The next landfall would be America, wouldn't it?"

Dan took a shopping bag from the car, out of which stuck the neck of a bottle of wine. "Not quite. Right across, it would be northern Canada. Labrador, to be exact."

"Oh." Megan turned from the view. "I was hoping it would be New York. Love that city."

"Me too." He handed her a plastic bag. "Here, I got some fresh prawns from the fish shop. Could you peel them while I get the barbeque going? That's just the starter. I got lamb cutlets for the main course."

"Sounds fantastic."

* * *

Half an hour later, they were sitting on the little beach below the cottage, eating lamb cutlets with their fingers and sipping wine from paper cups.

Megan nibbled the last of the meat from the cutlet. "Wonderful flavour. You're a good cook."

He shrugged. "Not my cooking. The lamb from this area has a very distinct flavour. Could be because the sheep graze all over the mountains, eating heather and grass."

Megan put the bone on the paper plate beside her. "That was all so delicious. The prawns, the lamb, the baked potato.

Thank you."

"More wine?" Without waiting for a reply, he leaned forward and filled her cup.

Leaning on her elbow, Megan stretched out on the blanket. "The sun has disappeared. I love this light, just before it gets really dark."

"The blue hour," Dan said. "Like in Paris. But here, it's even more magic."

"Yes."

They were quiet, lost in their own thoughts. Megan studied Dan surreptitiously, while he gazed out at sea. *A handsome man, fun and intelligent. Thoughtful and kind, someone I could easily fall in love with. So different from Stephen. And we have a lot more in common, like the same things, been to the same places. And we both know how this evening is going to end. But we're not rushing it. He's giving me a little space. That's considerate and generous.* She sipped the last of the wine. "Wonderful night, isn't it?" she murmured into the darkness. "Still so warm."

He turned to her. "Yes. How about a swim?"

"I didn't bring a swimsuit."

"No need. It's quite dark. Nobody around."

"True." On an impulse, she stood up and quickly stripped. "Let's go, then. Last one in is a wimpy chicken." Without waiting for a reaction, she ran down to the water and threw herself into the waves. The cool water was delicious on her hot skin. She lay back and floated, letting the waves bounce her body, slowly relaxing, the effect of the water igniting her senses in a strange way. Tiny, ice cold explosions in her private places made her feel nearly dizzy.

There was a splashing beside her. It was Dan, naked, frolicking in the waves. He came closer and their bodies joined under the water. They surfaced to kiss, his hands on her breasts. They stood up, gasping.

He laughed. "It's bloody freezing."

"We'd better get out, then." Megan waded out of the water and walked to the blanket and started to dry herself with a towel. By the time she was nearly dry, Dan had joined her.

Laughing, he shook his wet hair over her.

She squealed. "Stop it. You're like a wet dog!"

He grabbed her hand and pulled her toward the house. "Come on. Let's get inside and into bed. I'll warm you up."

"Is that a threat?" she giggled.

"It's a promise."

* * *

The bed was already made. Megan lay on the cool sheets and pulled the duvet over her. Dan joined her and cuddled up from behind. With his arms around her, his mouth on her neck, Megan felt a huge comfort, a sense of being loved. She closed her eyes, telling herself this was the best feeling in the world. Whatever happened next was of no importance.

He stirred and pressed his erection harder against her thighs. Delighted, she turned around. The kisses became more intense. His hands travelled to her breasts, and his fingers played with her nipples. She moaned softly and stroked his loins down to his groin until her fingers found their target. Not quite what she had hoped. But she didn't really mind. So he's petite in that area. Size doesn't matter…

He lay on top of her, pushed inside, then smiled. "Thanks for the welcome, sweet Megan."

She closed her eyes and kissed him. It was so lovely to lie here and get so close. But after a while, she slowly realised she felt more motherly than sexy. He seemed so hesitant, so slow and weak. Her libido evaporating, she found herself thinking of other things.

"Is this good for you?" Dan enquired with a small thrust.

"Oh, yes," she moaned. "Great." *Must get some furniture,*

she thought. "Oooh, that's fantastic." *Maybe that blue chair I saw in Dublin...* "Mmmm—oooh." *Is he going to finish soon?* "Oh, yesss..." *Curtains or blinds?*

It took him quite a long time to achieve a climax. Megan lay there, meeting his thrusts, moaning, making all the right noises, while mentally flicking through the IKEA catalogue. She had got to the bathroom section when he finally shouted, "Yes!"

Megan let out a final, long "Oooh."

Lathered with sweat, he collapsed on top of her. "Wasn't that..."

Megan sighed with relief. "Oh, yes. That was—"

"Amazing." He closed his eyes and fell asleep.

CHAPTER 9

While waiting to get the plumbing done, Megan decided to get stuck into cleaning up and doing any restoring she could manage herself. The electrician spent two days rewiring the house and the mess he left took several days to clean up. Megan had to borrow Beata's powerful vacuum cleaner to tackle all the fine dust that had settled everywhere. When the rewiring was finished and perfectly safe, she bought a new cooker and fridge. The plumbing side of things was a little tricky, but there was plenty of water in the stream. Lugging buckets upstairs was better than any workout, she told herself, but after a week of this, it lost its appeal. She called the plumber to ask if he could come sooner, but he was too busy to rearrange his schedule. The bucket regime would have to continue for a while longer. Megan told herself to look on the bright side—her arms would be more toned than after a year at the gym.

Boris helped out with the heavier work. Having worked on building sites in Russia, he had some very useful skills. "Your gutters are bad," he said. "If you get material, I can put them up." Which he did with astonishing speed. He also knew something about plastering and did a rough but solid job on the ceilings. The most helpful thing of all, he got two strong Ukrainian men to come and paint the outside of the house.

"That man's a gem," Megan said to Beata. "And if you don't want him, I know lots of women who would."

"Hands off," Beata said. "He's mine to work and torture when I need him."

"I'm beginning to understand why you stick to him like glue," Megan said. "But not why he sticks to you. Could it be love?"

"Shut up," Beata said with a warning glimmer in her eyes.

"Okay." Megan rolled her eyes and wondered yet again about this love-hate relationship. But she didn't worry about it much. She had her own love life to consider.

After the evening with Dan, Megan continued seeing him, mostly spending nights in his friend's cottage. The sex didn't improve, but she found herself enjoying their companionship and the long, beautiful evenings. They cooked together, walked on the beach, talked about books and travel. They laughed at silly jokes and hugged, kissed and fell into bed with the same results.

Despite the limp sex, it was a relationship Megan found comforting and enjoyable. Being part of a couple again was far better than going out alone. Dan's surfing friends turned out to be great company, and they often had parties on the beach after surfing, cooking sausages, drinking beer and singing silly songs to the tune of a guitar late into the night. *So the sex isn't much,* she told herself. *But it might improve ... and I'm not alone anymore. That's the most important part.*

Megan drove into Tralee when she had a day off and bought a carload of cleaning material, paint and brushes. Paudie arrived unannounced a few days later, "just to inspect the work in progress". He found Megan, halfway up a ladder, painting the living room wall.

"Well, look who's here," she said. "Hello, stranger. How are things with you?"

"Busy. This time of year always is. I came to look at

the bullocks, but then I saw the windows and doors open and thought I'd take a look. So, you're painting everything white?"

Megan put down the roller. "Yes. I like white walls and then lots of pictures. White makes a house so bright."

He nodded. "True." He looked up. "You painted the ceiling too. Hard work."

"It's awful. My arms were killing me. But that's all done now, even upstairs."

"That's a lot of work for a girl."

"For anyone, I'd think. But I have to do as much myself as I can. I had a glazier from Dingle town here earlier. He'll replace all the broken glass in the windows, but he said most of the window frames are rotten and need replacing." Megan sighed. "More money flying out of my bank account."

"Well, old houses eat money. If you want to stop the decay, you'll have to fork out the cash."

Megan put the roller in the tray. "I know. But it's a little painful at times." She shook her arms. "God, I'm stiff."

"Now you know what Michelangelo went through when he painted the Sistine Chapel. And he wasn't a girl."

Megan laughed. "No wonder he was always fighting with the Pope. Now, this girl wants a break. How about coffee?"

He helped her down from the ladder. "Sounds good. Could do with a break myself. Hang on. I'll lock Denis in the jeep."

"No, let him stay. We'll have coffee outside. It's such a lovely day."

Megan quickly made coffee and took it outside, where Paudie had settled into one of the new deckchairs, Denis at his feet. He got up to take the tray. "Here. Let me take that."

"Thanks. Put it on the table."

"Good coffee. The real stuff." Paudie remarked, taking a sip.

"I hate instant." Megan threw a piece of her biscuit at

Denis, who gobbled it up at once.

"Careful. Don't spoil that dog. He won't leave you alone now."

"I don't want him to." Megan scratched Denis behind the ear. He came closer and licked her hand.

Paudie laughed. "See? He's a sucker for a pretty girl."

"And I'm a sucker for a cute dog." She looked at him over the rim of her mug. "You look worn out."

He sat back and closed his eyes to the sun. "I had a sick cow. Had to get the vet. Then I stayed up all night to see if she'd pull through."

"Did she?"

"No. After all that, she died. Pity. One of my best breeders." He opened his eyes and drank some coffee. "But that's farming. Has its ups and downs. Mostly downs."

"Why did you come back here, then? Why get into farming at all? You seemed to like Vermont."

Paudie put his mug on the table. "To make a long story short, I came here when my dad got sick. Had to stay a long time. Then Dad died. I was going to sell the farm, but I had problems with my visa to the US. I had overstayed my visitor's visa and had no work permit. I couldn't go back. So I stayed here and then kept the farm going. And then, there was a woman…"

Megan settled deeper into the deck chair. "A woman? I know it's probably not my business, but—"

There was pain deep in Paudie's eyes as he looked at her. "No. None of your business. But for some reason, I don't mind telling you." He folded his arms and stared at the stream. "She was my… Don't know how to put it."

"Partner? Girlfriend?"

He shrugged. "Yes. All of that and more. American. A writer and journalist. Wrote for these fancy magazines. Vanity Fair. Stuff like that. She came here. Helped me nurse Dad. Then, when Dad died, she said she loved the place and made me do it up the way she liked it."

"Oh. I was wondering about the living room. She did that?"

Paudie grabbed his mug. "Yes. Don't go in there much myself now."

"So what happened?"

"She left."

Megan forgot about her coffee. "Oh. Why? Did you have a row?"

"No. She went back to Vermont to put her house on the market. Wanted to sell it and move over here permanently. We'd get married. But then, a month later, she phoned to say she wasn't coming back and she'd write to tell me why. Turns out she got cold feet or something. Didn't want to leave the good ol' US."

"Oh God. How terrible."

"Yeah."

"I'm sorry." Megan didn't know quite what to say.

"That's not all. She did come back two months later. But by then I had drowned my sorrows. Or tried to. She arrived without warning and found me—"

"Drunk?"

Paudie let out a sad little laugh. "If only that was all. No, I was shagging some bird I picked up in Tralee. My ex walked in without warning. Walked right out again, of course. Never knew why she came back, though. Haven't heard from her since."

"Oh shit."

"Yeah."

"How long ago was this?"

"Two years, I think. Something like that."

"Oh." Megan looked at Paudie. For some reason, they both started to laugh.

Paudie punched her shoulder. "That's right, laugh. It's kind of ridiculous when you think about it. If you'd witnessed it, you'd have been in stitches. There I was, stark bollock naked, humping away. The door opens and there she stands, wearing her white skirt and high heels, like Grace fucking Kelly."

"What happened then?"

"Everything. It was like a farce. Everyone screaming. Didn't take her long to get the hell out. And the poor bird I was with thought she was going to be killed by a wronged wife or something, so she took off as well." Paudie sighed and ran his hand over his face. "I was a little shell-shocked for a while."

"I can imagine," Megan giggled. "Looks like you're as unlucky in love as I am."

"Yeah," he sighed. "Haven't had much luck since."

"And Beata?"

"Smokes in bed."

"That's why you threw her out?"

He shot a look at Megan. "Is that what she said? That's not what happened. I asked her to quit, and she packed her stuff and was gone before we could sort it out."

"I take it you weren't compatible?" Megan suggested.

"If you want to use a fancy word. Tricky business," Paudie said. "Love, I mean."

"Sure is."

He glanced at her. "But you're seeing Dan Nolan."

"How did you know?"

"Just a wild guess. Saw you two at the pub a few weeks ago. You looked very cosy together. Thought you said you'd given up on men?"

Megan squirmed. "Well, it's… I'm just… He—"

"He managed to get through your wall of defence? Smooth operator."

"Doesn't sound as if you like him much."

Paudie laughed. "Like? No. I've seen him in action. Lawyers are a breed apart. Dan Nolan would convict his own granny to win a case."

"I've never seen that side of him."

Paudie lifted an eyebrow. "No? I'm sure he's hot stuff in private."

Megan blushed. "That's right." She wondered what Paudie would say if she told him that Dan was everything but hot in bed. If he knew that even though the sex wasn't what she had hoped, the rest of her relationship with Dan was soothing and loving, helping her to heal. He'd probably scoff at it. "I'm very happy with him," she said.

"That's good, then." Paudie got up. "Have to get going."

Megan scrambled to get out of the deckchair. "Yes, me too."

He grabbed her hand and pulled her to her feet. Their eyes met for an instant. Megan was the first to look away.

Paudie touched her shoulder. "Take care, girl. Don't let anyone walk on you. Least of all Dan Nolan." He strolled away with Denis at his heels.

* * *

"Five thousand," the man said.

Megan gulped. "That's the lowest price? For a septic tank? Oh God, I didn't believe it would be that much. I'll have to think about this."

The man shrugged. "Don't think too long. The old system is, if you forgive me, total crap. You'll have trouble if you don't update it."

"Shit."

"Yes, that's what you'll have. All over the garden if the stream decided to flood." He walked back to the front gate where his van was parked. He handed Megan a card. "Here's my number. Call me when you've made up your mind."

Megan sighed and took the card. "No need. I've made up

my mind. This has to be done. So, when can you come? The plumber will be here on Wednesday to replace the pipes, so…"

He consulted his diary. "Hmm, I haven't got a lot of jobs at the moment, so we could come on Tuesday. That way it'll be done in time for the plumber to connect the rest to the new tank."

"Brilliant." Megan mentally waved goodbye to her entire savings. "See you then."

He drove off, and Megan sank down on a deckchair, her legs shaking, wondering for the hundredth time if she was completely sane. With the electricity, plumbing and septic tank, more than ten thousand of her carefully saved euros would be gone. Oh well, it was only money. She had fifteen thousand left for her old age and the two months' severance pay. Plus the salary Beata was paying her and the dole money she collected every week. Enough to get by for a short while.

She looked up as she heard the gate open. A woman entered the garden and looked around. She shielded her eyes from the sun with her hand. "Hello?" she chanted. "Anyone home?"

Megan got up. "Yes. I'm here, by the back door."

"Oh." The woman approached. "Hello. You must be Megan. I'm Diana Connolly-Smith. From Hollyville House over there." She waved her hand in the direction of a clump of trees further up the road. "Should have come to say hello earlier, but two of our mares foaled at nearly exactly the same time, so I didn't get a chance until that was out of the way. You know what horses are like."

"Yes. I mean, no. Don't know much about horses." Megan held out her hand. "Hello. Nice to meet you."

Diana was tall and rangy with mousy brown hair in a messy bun and bright blue-green eyes in a youngish but weather-beaten face. Her handshake was firm, her gaze direct and her smile friendly. She wore riding boots, stained jodhpurs and a quilted waistcoat over a green man's shirt. "Sorry, should have changed my clothes, but I have to go back to see to the calves. Farming is a dirty business, don't you know?"

"I suppose."

"Anyway, just came to tell you that we'll be putting two mares and foals in the field here beside you tomorrow. Paudie is putting the sheep up the mountains, so he said I could put them here. Hope you don't mind."

"Of course not. I'd love to have them. Much prettier to look at than the scruffy old sheep anyway."

Diana smiled. "Absolutely, old girl. But they're my most valuable brood mares, so I needed a very sheltered spot for them."

"Great. Looking forward to seeing them."

Diana put her hands in her pockets and looked at Megan as if noticing her for the first time. "You're the image of your uncle. Handsome man, if a little girly in his looks. But on a woman, they sit perfectly."

"Thank you."

"So, you're doing up the house, then?"

Megan nodded and laughed. "Yes. For my sins. It gobbles up money, though."

"Yes. It would. Tough choice. Whether to sell it or not, I mean. Glad you're not. There've been O'Farrells in this area since time began, or for the past eight hundred years, anyway. The Connolly-Smiths are blow-ins compared to them. Only arrived here two hundred years ago. And our house is Victorian. Practically a new-build."

Megan smiled. "Yes, my house must be older than that. I think it was built at the beginning of the eighteenth century. But why don't you sit down? I'll make some tea."

Diana shook her head. "Thanks, pet, but I must get back. We're branding the calves today, so we need all hands on deck." She moved closer and touched Megan's arm. "I don't know if… well, I should tell you… if you're digging around in the house…"

Intrigued, Megan looked at Diana. "Yes?"

"Well, this will sound like complete nonsense. But I have reason to believe there's some sort of treasure hidden somewhere in the house." Diana looked around and lowered her voice. "Your Aunt Molly was friendly with my grandmother. She was from a Catholic family, and she and Molly were related. Unusual at the time for a Catholic girl to marry into a Protestant family."

"Yes," Megan agreed. "It must have caused a bit of a stir."

"You're right. It did. But anyway, that's beside the point. What I want to tell you is that Molly told Granny she found a box in the attic containing some jewellery. Old pieces from the time the house was built. Nothing big like a tiara or anything but family pieces. The O'Farrells were quite well off at the time. And one of the brides received a trousseau of some sort. I think there was a gold necklace and a Claddagh ring with a ruby in the middle of the heart."

Megan stared at Diana. "Really? But Claddagh rings are quite common."

"Normally, yes. But this one was an old ring made in Galway in the eighteenth century. One of the O'Farrell wives came from there. This one would be of great value."

"Wow. What did Molly do with them?"

Diana shrugged. "I don't know. She told Granny she would hide it away and make sure the Quinns got it. But then she died without making a will, and Pat got the lot. It was his anyway, of course."

"Yes. I suppose. But I doubt there's anything like that in the house. I've been all over it."

"She probably did sell it," Diana said, moving away. "Thought I'd tell you just in case, though."

"Of course. Thank you."

Diana winked. "Just between you and me, of course. But do be careful."

"How do you mean? Careful of what?"

"Oh," Diana said airily. "You never know who might be watching you."

* * *

"What did she mean?" Megan panted as she struggled to keep up with Paudie's giant strides up the mountainside. "Who might be watching me?

"Who knows? Diana's a bit of an eccentric at times. Heart of gold though."

"She was very nice. Hang on a minute."

Paudie stopped. "What's wrong?"

Megan looked up at his tall frame, silhouetted against the blue sky. He looked powerful there, at one with the steep green slopes of the mountains, the breathtaking views of the ocean and the cool clean breeze ruffling his black hair. "I need to catch my breath for a minute. We're not all mountain goats, you know."

Paudie laughed. "Thought you said you were fit?"

"Yes, I am. But not as fit as you, obviously." Megan looked down the narrow path winding up from the valley. "We've come quite a long way. And this is one hell of a steep slope."

Paudie scanned the incline above them. "We can rest up there, at the rocks. It's pretty sheltered, and we can have our lunch and take a break."

"About time." Megan wiped her forehead with the sleeve of her tee-shirt. "Have you spotted any of your sheep yet?"

"No. They usually go much higher in the summer." He pointed at the steep slope above. "See those white dots up there?"

Megan squinted in the bright light. "You mean those

little fluffy things? Are they your sheep?"

"I don't know. Can't tell until I'm closer. Mine have a blue patch on the back. It's quite a small flock, though. Come on, let's get to that rock. I can tell you need a rest."

Megan was relieved when they reached the rock. The flat surface made an ideal resting place. She eased off her new walking boots, took off her socks and wiggled her toes. She bit into the sandwich Paudie handed her. "Yummy. Sausage sandwich. I used to make them in college." She lay back on the rock and closed her eyes. "Best part of the walk."

"If you hadn't decided to break in your new walking boots today, you'd be more comfortable."

Megan sat up and rubbed her feet. "What choice did I have? I never owned a pair of walking boots before."

Paudie handed her a bottle of water. "Didn't know you were such a townie. Walking is the best exercise there is."

"Especially here." Megan looked at the view while she drank. "Thanks for bringing lunch. I wouldn't be able to carry anything up these steep paths. What else do you have in that rucksack?"

"Nothing much. Just the food and water and some raingear. Brought a jacket for you too. Didn't think you'd have the brains to think of that."

"You know me so well already."

Paudie picked up his binoculars. "You're easy to read." He scanned the mountainside. "Good. I can see them, right up there, by the ridge. Oh, and look! An eagle."

Megan sat up. "What? Really? Didn't know there were any here."

"They released about half a dozen into the wild a few years ago. Some died of poisoning but a couple survived and are breeding. This one's big. Must be the male. Want to see it?"

"Yes, of course. Stop hogging the binoculars." Megan went to sit beside Paudie.

He gave her the binoculars. "Over there, right above the ridge."

She lifted the binoculars to her eyes. But all she could see was blue sky. "Where? I can't see him. He must be gone."

Paudie put both his arms around her and took the binoculars. He held them to her eyes and guided her slowly to the right angle. "There. Hold still. Look."

Then she saw it. The eagle. Black, with a lighter head. With his huge wingspan, the eagle hovered over the edge of the mountain, turning his head to one side, then the other, scanning the valley. He stayed there, completely still, until he flapped his wings and glided away across the sky. Circled by Paudie's arms, Megan watched the eagle until it was only a black speck.

She turned to him. "How beautiful. Such a privilege to see it. Aren't we lucky?"

Paudie looked at Megan without replying. They were so close, she could feel his warm breath on her face and smell the soap he used. "Yes," he said quietly. "We're very lucky indeed."

With a surge of affection, Megan kissed him on the cheek. "Thanks for bringing me. I know I'm a pain and I slow you down."

Paudie put his binoculars into the rucksack. "You're not a pain. And I have the time. Better to walk slowly on such a grand day."

She inched away on the rock, sensing his discomfort. *What just happened? Is there…?* She shook her head. *No. We're just friends. I'm getting so close to Dan. But…*

"What are you sitting there shaking your head and muttering to yourself about?" Paudie teased. "You look like an auld woman doing some kind of witching spell."

Megan laughed. She got to her feet and brushed off the seat of her jeans. "That's right. I put a curse on you."

"Thought so. Or maybe you were wishing I'm Dan

Nolan?"

"Of course not. Anyway, he's busy today. Had to spend the day in court, he said."

"Rather him than me. Reminds me why I prefer farming to an office job, despite the hard work."

Megan laughed and looked up at the sky. "Oh, yes. Couldn't think of a better place to be on such a day. Especially when I had the day off and they're installing the septic tank. So your invitation came at the right moment."

"Glad you could come." Paudie stood up and hitched up his rucksack. "Enough slacking. We have to get up a little higher before it starts to rain."

"Rain? Where?"

"There." He pointed westward, where dark clouds gathered. "It'll be coming here in about twenty minutes."

"We'd better get going, then." Megan looked around. "But where's Denis? He was here just a minute ago. I thought he'd be begging for my sandwich."

"You're right. Don't know where he got to. Here, Denis!" Paudie called. "Come here, you fool!"

His call was answered by a howl, followed by a whimpering.

Paudie looked around. "What was that? Sounds like he's in trouble."

"It's coming from over there." Megan pointed above them. "Behind that rock. Sounds like he's hurt."

They scrambled up to the rock. The whimpering was stronger now, more pitiful. Megan turned the corner and saw Denis trying to pull his front leg out of a metal contraption.

"Oh, fuck." Paudie got on his knees. "He's stuck in a trap. Look, his leg is torn to shreds." Paudie pulled at the trap. Denis howled and tried to bite him. "Megan, hold him while I get his leg out," Paudie ordered.

Megan fell onto her knees. Avoiding Denis' snapping

teeth, she managed to hold his head away from Paudie while he opened the trap and pulled it off the dog's leg.

"There," Paudie sighed. "It's off."

"Thank God. You've strong hands." Megan let go of Denis who whimpering and crying, started to lick Paudie's face. "Look, he's saying thank you."

Paudie pushed the dog away and examined the leg that was bleeding profusely. "We have to stop the bleeding." He pulled off his shirt and started to rip strips off it. "This will do." He wrapped the strips tightly around Denis' leg. "I'll have to carry him down and then get to the vet. Can you take the rucksack, Megan?"

They slowly made their way down the mountainside. It was steep in parts, and Megan had to look away from the sheer drop at one side of the path. Paudie, with Denis slung across his bare shoulders, walked swiftly ahead. The dark clouds rolled in over them. It started to rain.

"Do you want your jacket?" Megan called.

"No, we have to keep walking. Can't stop now."

The rain quickly changed from steady drizzle to torrential downpour. Megan stopped and pulled the jackets out of the rucksack. She ran ahead, caught up with Paudie and draped one of the anoraks across the dog and Paudie's naked shoulders. "There. Should keep some of it off you."

He stopped briefly and turned around. "Thanks." His eyes scanned her wet body. "Put one on yourself. You're drenched."

Megan looked down. Noticing her tee-shirt clinging to her breasts, she quickly threw on the jacket. "Won't do much good."

"Better than nothing." He started walking again, increasing his speed when they reached the foot of the mountain.

When they were on the flat, they half ran the last half mile to Paudie's house. Once inside, he threw Megan a towel. "Here, go and have a hot shower while I see to the dog."

She caught the towel. "Thanks." She headed for the bath-room, the hot water like a mirage in her mind. But before she got there, a ringing noise from the kitchen stopped her. *My phone. Shit.* Shivering, she turned around and went to answer it.

"Hello?"

"Miss O'Farrell?"

"Yes?"

"Declan Murphy here. Septic tank. We've nearly fin-ished."

"Oh, great."

He paused. "But we found something."

"A problem?"

"No," he said. "It's something else."

Irritated, Megan peeled her wet tee-shirt away from her body. "Yes? What? Come on, tell me."

"You better come down here and see for yourself."

CHAPTER 10

"What could it be?"

"Uh, a dead body?" Paudie said darkly.

"Very funny. Of course it isn't. They'd have called the cops if that was the case."

Paudie wiggled his eyebrows. "Well, you never know what lurks beneath old houses."

"Stop it, Paudie, there's nothing like that there. But I wonder what it could be?"

"The only way to find out is to go down there and see."

"Of course." Megan grabbed the plastic bag with her wet clothes. "I'm going now."

"Sure you're warm enough?"

Megan laughed and hitched up the baggy trousers. "Warm? Yes. Fashionable? No. But you never know. Old corduroys held up by binder twine and a scratchy sweatshirt might be the latest rage very soon."

"If you keep wearing it around town, I wouldn't be surprised." Paudie drained his cup and put it on the kitchen table. "I'm taking Denis to the vet. Sure you'll be okay?"

"Of course. You must get him seen to. He probably needs an antibiotic." Megan patted Denis in his basket by the stove. "You'll be all right." The dog lifted his head and whimpered. He licked her hand and put his head on his paws with a long sigh.

"He'll milk this for all it's got," Paudie said. "We'll have a martyr on our hands, just you see."

"Why not? He had a terrible shock, poor fellow."

"Yes, but he'll live." Paudie put on his jacket. "Let me know what they found at your house when you get there."

"Of course. I'll call you. Got to get down there now to see if they've finished. And then the plumber is coming tomorrow to rip everything apart. That job will take most of this week."

"Are you staying with Beata while they're doing it?"

Megan stopped on her way to the door. "No. Why?"

"You can't stay in your house while they're ripping up the pipes. Won't be very comfortable."

"But I'll be out all day working at Beata's," Megan argued.

"Yes, but even spending the night will be hell. All doors open, floorboards taken up…" He glanced at Megan. "Why don't you come and stay here? In my spare room, just for the few nights?"

Megan hesitated. "Thanks. Okay, why not? I won't make much noise and stay in my room."

"I'll hold you to that," Paudie laughed.

* * *

It had stopped raining by the time Megan reached the house. A van and a small digger stood in front of the gate. She pulled in behind them, jumped out of the car, and ran around the house, hardly noticing the ragged lawn was now like a ploughed field, the green grass replaced by piles of black earth. She bumped into a man coming out of the shed. Declan Murphy, the septic tank man.

She stopped. "Hi. Sorry. I was in such a rush."

He nodded. "Evening. We're just about finished. We'll

just close up some of the holes."

"Okay," Megan panted. "Fine. Great. But what about that thing you found? What is it? Is it serious?"

He laughed. "No, don't worry. It was just something we came across when we dug beside the shed. But let me show you what we've done first." He walked toward the fence at the side. "The tank is here. And the inspection hole right beside it. You have great percolation here. So from an environmental point of view, it's much better than the old one."

Megan nodded. "Oh. That's good."

"Yup. Sorry about the garden, but all you have to do is rake it over and throw some grass seed on it, and it'll come up in no time."

"Great."

"I'll get my mate to give me a hand, and then we'll be gone in about half an hour. I'll send you the invoice in a couple of days."

"Thanks."

"We put the stuff we found on the kitchen table. And thanks for the tea and sandwiches you left us."

"You're welcome." Megan hitched up her trousers and walked into the kitchen, where she found a parcel wrapped in dirty newspaper on the table. After peeling off many layers, she discovered what was inside. A leather pouch with the letter M in faded gold. With shaking hands, she opened the pouch. Inside were two small wooden boxes. She opened the first one. Her breath caught in her throat. A necklace. Gold filigree studded with semi-precious stones, black with age. It would be beautiful, once cleaned up. She put it back in the box and opened the smaller one.

Although sure of what she would find, she nevertheless felt a mounting excitement as she caught sight of the content. A gold ring with two hands holding a heart wearing a crown. The O'Farrell Claddagh ring. Ignoring the dirt, she slipped it on her finger. It fit perfectly.

* * *

"What's a Claddagh ring?" Beata asked. "I've seen them, but I never knew the significance of them. I love the design of the two hands around the heart. But why is the heart wearing a crown?"

Megan studied the ring. Now cleaned, it looked beautiful on the third finger of her right hand. The heart had a small ruby, and the crown was outlined with tiny diamonds. She had cleaned it with soap and water under the tap and carefully brushed the diamonds with her toothbrush until they sparkled. "I think it's to do with the saying 'let love and friendship reign'," she said.

"Yes. Makes sense." Beata looked at the ring. "It's lovely. Never seen such a beautiful one. Not like the crappy ones they sell in tourist shops."

"No. This is a very old one. Believed to have been made in Galway in the eighteenth century by someone called Joyce. He was the one who came up with the original design." Megan took off the ring and handed it to Beata. "If you look inside, you'll see a faded stamp with an anchor and the letters R and I. That's the mark of a Joyce ring."

Beata put the ring on her little finger. "Too small for me. You have tiny fingers."

"Strange how it fits me."

Beata handed back the ring. "Isn't there a special way to wear it?"

Megan slipped the ring back on her finger, where it felt as if it belonged. "Yes. Traditionally, if the owner of the ring wears it with the crown pointing towards the fingernail, he or she is said to be in love or married. To wear the ring with the heart pointing to the fingernail, he or she is said to be unattached to anyone."

Beata glanced at Megan's hand. "It says you're unattached. But I thought—"

Megan shrugged. "I don't want anyone getting ideas."

* * *

"It was a parcel with an old necklace and the O'Farrell Claddagh ring," Megan told Paudie later that night when he phoned. "It was in a leather pouch marked with the letter M in gold. That would be Molly, I suppose."

"No, I don't think so. It's probably one of the O'Farrell women. They were all called either Mary, Maureen or a derivative of Mary. I think there were one or two Margarets too."

"I see. I wonder when Molly hid this, though."

"Why don't you look at the date on the newspaper it was wrapped in?"

"Of course. Why didn't I think of that?"

"Because you're not as clever as me," Paudie said. "When are you coming over?"

"Tomorrow evening. I have to be here when the plumber arrives, and then I'll go over to Beata's. I'll come back here to check on their progress later and get my stuff. Then I'll be at your place around seven. That okay?"

"Yes, that's fine."

"I have a date with Dan later, so I'll be out all night."

"Fine."

"How's Denis?" Megan asked.

But Paudie had hung up.

* * *

The date on the old newspaper the parcel was wrapped in was difficult to make out. But the year said 1940. *Dad would have been two*, Megan thought. *Maybe around the time Molly found out about his existence… Maybe that's why she hid the jewellery.*

She didn't have time to think about it, however, as she had a busy day ahead of her. She hid the box with the necklace under the old bellows. The ring would stay on her finger for good. It felt like hers, as if her female ancestors, all the way from eighteenth-century Galway, wanted her to wear it.

When her phone rang, she thought it would be Beata or Dan, but a female voice asked if this was Megan O'Farrell.

"Yes, I'm Megan. How can I help you?"

"This is Maria Slattery from Social Welfare."

"Oh. Hello."

"I'm calling to enquire if it's true that you're working part time at a B and B called The Blue Door?"

Megan swallowed. How on earth had they found out? Beata paid her in cash, and she hadn't mentioned it to anyone when she went to collect her unemployment benefit. "Uh…"

"If this is true, I'm calling to give you a warning. You can't work anywhere, either full-time or part-time while drawing unemployment payments. This is a serious offense you know."

"But… the dole money is puny," Megan protested. "How could anyone be expected to live on that?"

"That's beside the point," The woman snapped. "I could report you, and then you'd have to go to court."

"How did you find out?"

"I can't tell you that. It's confidential."

Megan gritted her teeth. "So, someone squealed on me, is that it?"

"Let's say it was a hint." Maria Slattery's tone softened. "Not a very nice thing to do, I agree. But there you are, people aren't nice. Tralee is a small town and people talk."

"I don't live in Tralee," Megan argued.

"No, but you live in the catchment area. Everyone comes

into Tralee to go to the bank and shop and things like that."

"I see. So, what am I going to do?"

"Stop drawing unemployment," Mary Slattery said. "Or quit your part-time job. The choice is up to you. I won't report you if you sort this out at once." There was a click as she hung up.

Megan stood there by the window, staring blindly at the view. Who could have reported her? Everyone knew she worked at The Blue Door, but very few knew about her drawing the dole. Maybe someone had spotted her going into the Social Welfare office? *Oh shit! I'm just going to stop drawing the dole. It's a pittance anyway.*

A thought struck Megan. Maybe it was a hoax? Only one way to find out. She looked up the Social Welfare office on her smartphone and dialled the number. "Is there a Maria Slattery in your office?" she asked when the receptionist replied.

"Yes. Do you want to speak to her?"

Megan hesitated. "Yes please."

"Just a moment and I'll connect you. She might be out, but then you can leave a message on her voicemail."

There was a click and a brief silence. Then a woman's voice Megan recognised: "This is Maria Slattery. I'm away from my desk but please leave a message and I'll call you back as soon as I can."

Megan hung up. It was no hoax. Someone had told on her.

By now used to the sound of farm machinery, the rumble of a tractor barely registered as Megan tidied up. The plumbers were due to arrive any minute, so she had to make sure the kitchen was tidy and there were no obstacles for the work ahead.

The rumble hadn't registered. But the smell did. Foul. Stinking. Choking. *Not again. I must try to get used to it or it will drive me insane*, Megan told herself. But this time the stench was so strong, it felt as if the slurry had been sprayed directly into the house. Holding her breath, Megan went outside. A tractor with a slurry tank was just pulling out from the field beside the house. The field where the foals were to go was no longer green.

"Hey!" Megan shouted and waved at the tractor. "Stop! Who told you to—" But the tractor drove down the road without stopping.

* * *

"Oh, no," Diana moaned from the driver's seat of her jeep. "I can't unload the horses now. This'll take over a week to be fit for grazing."

"Thought so," Megan said. "I was going to call you but didn't have your number."

"Who did this?"

"The contractor down the road. Said he had orders from Paudie. But when I spoke to him, he said no. He didn't tell anyone to spray the fields, as he knew you were coming to put your horses here."

Diana's eyes narrowed. "We have to get to the bottom of this. It must have been malicious. Is someone trying to get you to sell?"

Megan sighed. "Just about everyone. Beata thinks I'm nuts. Dan thinks I should sell and buy a smaller place. The Quinn brothers are leaning on me, saying they'll make me an offer. Paudie—" She thought for a moment. "Actually, he hasn't said anything at all. He's the only one who leaves me alone."

"Very restful person, really, isn't he?" Diana looked at Megan's hand. "Oh! You found it. The ring. Let me have a look."

Megan took off the ring. "Yes. They found it when they

dug the hole for the new septic tank. It was so dirty, I didn't know what it was at first. I found the necklace too. It's beautiful."

Diana studied the ring. "Gorgeous. A bit rough but that's because it's so old. Here, put it back on. But are you sure you should be wearing it all the time like this? I mean, is it safe?"

Megan put the ring back on her finger. "I don't care. It feels as if I've worn it always. I feel naked without it."

Diana glanced at it. "But you're not wearing it the right way. If you're attached…"

"I'm not. Well, as you know I'm seeing someone but I don't feel 'attached' to him. Yet."

Diana nodded. "Quite right. Take it slowly, and make sure it's the real thing. The ring is beautiful. Maybe it'll bring you luck." She started the engine of the jeep. "Okay, I'll take these horses back home. We can have a look again in a couple of days. Pity. The grass is so sweet here."

There was thumping sound from the horsebox attached to the jeep. "Please," Megan said. "Can I see the foal?"

Diana switched off the engine. "Okay, why not? Open the front door of the box and you can have a peek. But be careful. That mare nips a bit."

Megan walked to the horsebox and carefully opened the little door at the front. The grey mare pushed her muzzle toward Megan's outstretched hand and let out a small snort. Beside her, the black foal looked on with wide eyes. "Hello," Megan whispered, touching the silky coat. The foal sniffed at her hand, then hid behind his mother. The mare looked back at him, then gave Megan's hand a little shove, as if to say 'enough peeking'. Megan breathed in the smell of hay and horse and withdrew her head. She closed the door with a little sigh of regret. "Thanks," she said to Diana, standing beside her. "They're beautiful."

Diana put the catch back on the door. "Hard work but

worth it. When you breed a winner, it's better than winning a million euros in the lotto. But that doesn't happen very often, of course. It's the beef cattle that make our living. These beautiful creatures are less of a certainty. But horses are my first love. Don't make me much money. We just about break even, but what a bore life would be without them." She shook herself. "Enough blathering. Got to go. Don't worry about this. It'll be okay in a couple of days. Especially if it rains. You can always be sure it will here."

"That's true."

A blue van with a plumber's logo on the side drove up and pulled in behind Diana. The driver leaned his head out the window. "Morning! Can we drive in through the gate and park at the back door? Easier to get the material in that way. If that jeep and horsebox aren't going to stay, that is."

"Of course," Megan replied. "I'll be with you in a minute."

"Thanks." The driver wrinkled his nose. "Holy Mary, the slurry's bad today. What did they use? Extra strength?"

"Yeah." Megan sighed. "They nuked it."

"I'd better get going. See you soon, love." Diana waved and expertly backed the jeep and horsebox into the road and drove off.

The van pulled in through the gate. Megan got ready for her day at The Blue Door as the plumbers didn't waste any time ripping out pipes and boring holes in the walls.

She left the smell and noise behind her and drove down the road towards Castlegregory, her mind on all that had happened during the morning. *Who is it? Who is doing their best to get me to leave?"*

* * *

"Who could have reported me?" Megan asked Beata the next

morning. "Only Dan and Paudie know about me collecting dole. And neither of them would have told on me."

Beata shrugged. "Who knows? My bet is on the Quinn brothers. They might have seen you. Or one of their friends or something."

Megan stuffed a sheet into the washing machine. "I think you're right. And then the slurry yesterday. That was done maliciously. A ploy to make me sell the house."

"Of course. Houses around here are like gold dust these days. And yours is a gem. There isn't a square foot available for rent during the summer months here. If you don't sell, you could make a lot of money renting out your place in July and August next year."

Megan looked at Beata. "Yes. That's true. I might consider that. If I find somewhere to stay during those months. Or I could always go to Dublin and stay with my mother for a few weeks at least."

"If you can bear it."

* * *

She hadn't come to any conclusion by the end of that day. Having packed a bag with enough clothes for a few days, she drove to Paudie's house, still trying to figure out who was trying to drive her out.

She forgot all about it when she got out of the car. The haunting sound of a melody being played on a flute hung in the still air. Paudie sat on the stone wall of the little back garden, playing his tin whistle, lost to the world around him.

She couldn't take her eyes off him. He was so still, so complete, somehow. Denis, his leg bandaged, lay at his master's feet. The mountains rising above the fields, against the sky tinged with pink, made the perfect backdrop.

Megan stood, listening to the music, taking in the scene. She didn't want to move or talk, didn't want this moment to end.

Paudie stopped playing and lifted his face to the sky. Then Megan saw his tears.

CHAPTER 11

Megan inched back to her car, got in and gently closed the door. After waiting a few minutes, she opened the door again and shouted, "Hello!"

Paudie ran his hand over his face. Smiling at Megan, he jumped off the wall. "Hi there. Are you here already? I sat here, fiddling around with some music."

"I didn't know you played the tin whistle."

He looked at the little metal flute in his hand. "Yeah. Learned to play when I was about seven. My mother taught me. She was very much into Irish music. She had a lovely voice."

"Maybe you'll play me a tune sometime?"

He put the tin whistle in his pocket. "Maybe. But not that one."

"It reminded you of your mother?" Megan asked as gently as she could.

Paudie nodded. "Yes. Funny how it always brings me back to her. She died when I was twenty. Long time ago now, but…"

Megan took his hand. "I know. I lost my dad a few years ago. I'll never stop missing him. Were you close to your mother?"

"Yes." He straightened his shoulders, as if to rid himself of sad thoughts. "You have to turn your mind away when you get into that kind of mood. So we won't talk about it anymore." He took her bag. "I put some sheets in the spare room behind the kitchen. It's nice and warm from the stove and very quiet."

"Great." She patted Denis. "How is he? I see he isn't putting that paw down at all."

"No, he's a little bit sore. The vet stitched the wound and gave him antibiotics. He'll be all right in a few days. But go on, you'll be late. Is Nolan picking you up?"

Megan picked up her pace. "Yes. He'll be here in about twenty minutes."

The room was small, bare and clean. The wrought-iron bed had a thick mattress covered with a quilt of many colours. The rest of the furniture consisted of an old chest of drawers with brass knobs, a chair and hooks on the wall for hanging clothes. The window overlooked the little garden at the back. Megan took the sheets and made the bed. She grabbed the towel hanging on the wall and tiptoed to the bathroom. After a quick shower, she padded back to her room to get ready for the evening with Dan.

When she came into the kitchen, she found Paudie at the table with a laptop. He looked up. "All bright-eyed and bushy-tailed, I see. Not quite the outfit for an evening on the town, though."

Megan glanced down at her jeans and runners. "We're going to the beach. There'll be some big waves at the back beach this evening, they said. With good wind for windsurfing and kite surfing too. So there's a lot going on."

"And you'll be watching the show?"

"Yes. And then we'll have a picnic with the others. It's great fun. People from all over Europe are here this weekend." She glanced at his computer. "What are you doing? Another kind of surfing?"

He looked at the screen. "No. I'm doing my accounts and looking up *The Irish Field*. I'm not into that Facebook stuff.

But I'm sure you have a large following."

Megan shrugged. "Used to. I've kind of forgotten about the Internet since I came here. Haven't even switched on my laptop. It's as if it would break the spell."

He looked up at her. "The spell?"

"Yes. We seem so far away from all that stuff here. The Internet. Twitter. Facebook. Doesn't seem important or relevant. I don't even watch TV. I listen to the news on my little radio, but sometimes I even forget to do that. The world outside Dingle doesn't seem to matter much."

Paudie smiled and shook his head. "You're turning into a real Kerrywoman. But when winter comes, you'll change your mind. The winter storms will force you indoors. Then you'll have to think of some way to amuse yourself."

"Maybe." She sat down at the table and propped her chin in her hands. "But then I could take up weaving or knitting Aran sweaters. Those traditional Irish knits are very popular all over the world. I might even sell them on eBay. Or I might just get stuck into the books I've been promising myself to read."

"That should keep you busy." He cocked his head "Is that Nolan's car outside?"

Megan didn't stir. "Probably. I'll be off in a minute."

"Letting him wait, are we?" Paudie winked. "Not letting him think you're that eager?"

Megan laughed. "Yeah, why not? 'Treat 'em like shit,' Beata says. Not you," she added, putting a hand on his arm. "You're my friend."

He put his hand on hers. "And you're mine, Meg. Don't you ever forget that."

The door opened. They looked up as Dan entered, a gush of cold air blowing in behind him.

There was a long silence. Then, without getting up or letting go of Megan's hand, Paudie spoke. "Evening, Mr Nolan, sir. What brings you to my humble abode?"

Ignoring Paudie, Dan looked at Megan. "Are you ready? We have to get going. The surf's up and everyone's waiting."

The tension was palpable in the kitchen. Megan could see Paudie's jaw tightening. She got up. "Yes. I'm ready."

Dan took a step back. "Okay. Let's go, then. Come on."

"Ordering the lady around, Mr Nolan?" Paudie's voice was as smooth as silk. "I don't think she takes to being bossed."

"Is that any of your business, Paudie O'Shea?"

Confused by the hostility, Megan looked from one the other. What was going on? With a feeling a fight was in the air, she got up, grabbed her sweater from a chair and walked to the door. She took Dan's arm. "Come on, we're late."

Still glaring at Paudie, Dan reluctantly followed her through the door.

"Bye, Paudie," Megan called over her shoulder.

"Don't wait up," Dan added, his voice dripping with irony. "We'll probably be very late."

"What was that all about?" Megan asked when they drove off.

Dan changed gears with unnecessary force, making the gearbox screech. "Nothing," he said between his teeth. "Except some stuff that will never get buried."

* * *

Megan took off her shoes and slowly opened the back door. She peered inside and listened. All was quiet. Denis slept on his blanket by the stove, but lifted his head as she padded inside. He wagged his tail but didn't get up.

Megan put her hand on his head. "Shh, we don't want to wake Paudie."

Denis yawned and closed his eyes. "Good boy," Megan whispered, and tiptoed out of the kitchen. She made her way down the corridor toward the guest room, slipping out of her jacket as she went. Yawning, she pulled off her sweater and started to unbutton her shirt. Exhausted after a long evening of talking, singing, laughing and walking on the beach, she just wanted to get in between the sheets, put her head on the pillow and go to sleep. It had been a fun evening, which ended with a long kissing session in Dan's car just outside the gates. It was as if he was willing Paudie to come out and find them there. But nothing happened and Megan finally pulled away.

She put her fingers to her lips, where the warmth of his kisses still lingered. He may not be such a great lover but he's a hell of a kisser, she thought sleepily. Her shirt open, she was just about to open the door to her room, when there was a noise further down the corridor. She turned her head and discovered Paudie, naked except for his pyjama pants, coming out of the bathroom.

He stopped in his tracks. "Well, hello, there. What time do you call this?"

Megan looked at her watch. "It's one thirty in the morning."

He lifted one eyebrow. "That's a little late, isn't it? Or early if you prefer."

"I suppose. But so what? We had fun. Then we went on talking in the car."

Paudie came closer. "Talking?" He peered at her. "Is that why you have a hickey on your neck?"

Megan felt her face redden. "Don't know what you mean." She put her hand to her neck. "It's a scratch from a branch. Must have happened when we were walking…"

"Oh yes," Paudie drawled. "Must have."

He was now so close Megan could feel his warm breath on her face and smell the soap he used. His naked chest nearly touched her breasts. She pulled at her shirt and inched away, her breathing oddly laboured and her face hotter still. "Well, I think it's time for bed…"

He didn't move. "Yes," he murmured. "Maybe it is."

Rooted to the spot, Megan found herself mesmerised by the look in his eyes and the sheer nearness of him. "Good night," she whispered as she slowly came to her senses.

He touched her face. "Good night. Sweet dreams." He disappeared into his room and closed the door.

Megan stood there for a while, trying to get her breathing back to normal and her legs to obey her. *What happened? What was that all about?* She shook her head. He was probably just tired and perhaps a little drunk. They'd be back to normal in the morning.

Finally in bed, she was aware of Paudie's presence in the next room, and in her thoughts.

* * *

When the plumbers were finished, Megan moved back into her house. She missed Paudie's company, but being away from his sharp eyes and his quick assessment of her moods was a relief. She also had a feeling there had been a slight shift in their relationship, which made her feel uncomfortable.

"Are you sure you don't want to stay another few days?" he asked when he saw her packing up.

"No thanks. I have to be there when the glazier comes to do the windows, and then my house will be more weatherproof and more comfortable. I have to learn to live on my own there, Paudie."

He nodded. "Very true. I'll miss your chatter though."

"I'll miss you too. But I'm only down the road, so we'll see each other often all the same."

She drove off, leaving him standing at the gate, looking a little forlorn.

The B and B was full and Megan had to spend extra hours

helping out and taking bookings on Beata's computer. Boris had become lazy and uncooperative, which made Beata bad-tempered and impatient.

"He's never here in the evenings anymore," she complained. "I don't know where he goes, and I don't care, but now I have to do all the boring chores myself. And then I'm so exhausted, I don't even wake up when he crawls into bed."

"Have you asked him where he goes?" Megan said.

Beata nodded. "Yes. He just says he's doing something important for himself." She shrugged. "I don't know what he means. I don't really understand the way Russians think."

"I'm sure he'll explain it one day." Megan turned back to the computer, where she was checking e-mails for new bookings.

"Yeah. Maybe." Beata resumed emptying the dishwasher then stopped and looked at Megan bleakly. "But what if he's doing some kind of extra job to save money for a ticket back to Russia? What will I do then?"

"Why do you say that? And why would you care? You act as if you hate him most of the time."

Beata shrugged. "I know and I do. But he's so handy to have around, you know?"

Megan smirked. "Yeah, right. You have no feelings for him at all?"

"I don't. None at all."

"Oh yeah?"

"Please. Stop going on about it." Beata clattered the dishes. "How are things with you? Danny boy still wonderful?"

"Haven't seen him much, to be honest. But I've been so busy here and with the house, I haven't much time to go out."

"I saw him at the pub with an older man last night."

Megan looked up. "Oh? That must be his dad."

"Yes. They look alike. The dad is handicapped or something. Walked in using a cane. They seemed to get on really well."

Megan stared at Beata. "Handicapped? I didn't know. Dan doesn't talk about him much. In fact, he seems to avoid the subject when I mention it. But... but doesn't his father run an estate agency?"

Beata closed the washing machine. "So? Can't he do that even if he can't walk? Can't be that much to do these days. Not many houses for sale. Must be hard to live on what he makes. Especially if he's handicapped."

"Must be," Megan mumbled and went back to the bookings on the screen. But she couldn't focus on them for a long time.

* * *

"Do you want to come to the races on Sunday?" Paudie asked when he dropped in with a sweater Megan had left behind.

"The races?"

"Yes, you know, where a bunch of horses run against each other and we place bets and cheer and drink beer and have a good time. The races."

Megan snatched the sweater from him. "I know what the bloody races are. I was just a little surprised that you'd go there."

Paudie leaned on the gate. "Why? I do go out for a bit of fun sometimes, you know. In any case, Diana has a horse in one of the races, so I thought we'd go and cheer her on. And this is the biggest event of the year here. Because of the Rose of Tralee festival. Very glamorous."

"The Rose of Tralee? Gosh, I had totally forgotten that was on."

Paudie shook his head mockingly. "You really are on another planet these days. Tralee is buzzing right now. Not that I'm interested in that sort of thing, but it's kind of fun all the same."

"But it's just a beauty pageant, isn't it?"

"In a way, yes. But I think it's much more than that. All these Irish girls from all over the world coming back to their roots. They're not just judged on their looks but on their personality and talent as well. Most of them are so wholesome and sweet. Yeah, okay, it's kind of cheesy. But it's so very Irish."

Megan laughed. "That's for sure. So, you've been watching? Who's your favourite to win?"

"The girl from Texas. She has a certain sassiness combined with Irish-girl-next-door sweetness." He winked. "Just like you."

Megan felt her face go pink. "Didn't know the girl-next-door was your type."

"I don't have a type. So, how about it? You want to go? Or do you have plans with Mr Nolan?"

"No, not this Sunday. He's in a surfing competition. So, yes, I'd love to. Sounds like fun. What'll I wear?"

Paudie laughed "The first question a woman ever asks, even if it's her own funeral. How about my old corduroys with the binder twine? You looked cute in those." He ruffled her hair. "I'll pick you up at one. See you then, kiddo."

CHAPTER 12

Tralee racecourse was packed. When Megan saw the crowds, the multi-coloured tents, the banners and flags, she realised what a special day it was. The newly crowned Rose of Tralee would be attending, and there would be a parade with all the contestants in vintage cars. The biggest race was Owen McCarthy Claims Specialists Handicap Steeplechase over two and a half miles, and everyone expected a great contest between the best thoroughbreds in the country.

"What a perfect day for the races," Megan said to Paudie as they went through the turnstile.

Paudie squinted at the sun. "It's a grand day. End of August is normally good, though. And so many of the farmers here have finished saving hay and all the crops. This year, they got two cuts of silage as well. So you'll see a lot of money changing hands." He glanced down at her. "You look nice."

Megan laughed. "Typical. I've made a huge effort to dress just right for the races and dug out my very expensive Prada dress, a remnant of my former life. I even went to the trouble of ironing it. And all you can say is 'nice.'"

"Oh. Okay." He looked at her again. "Your dress—excuse me, *Prada* dress—with that exquisite pattern of blue flowers, the sexy short skirt, teamed with—" he looked at her feet, "blue sandals with sky-high heels and a matching—no, wait, not matching—enormous handbag is the epitome of the well-dressed Kerrywoman at the races." He drew breath. "Better?"

"It would be if you meant it."

"I do. With bells and whistles."

"Yeah, right," Megan laughed.

"But what the hell is a Prada dress?"

"Prada is a very well-known designer."

"I see. You coulda fooled me. I thought it was some kind of weird material." He looked at her hand. "I see you're wearing the ring. But isn't it the wrong way around?"

"No, it isn't. I don't feel attached yet."

"Or in love?" he asked airily.

She thought for a moment. Was she in love with Dan? He made her feel happy and she liked him a lot. She was very attracted to him but love might have been too big a word. "Well, let's call it 'in like' for now," she replied. "Very much so, actually."

"Sounds complicated."

She shook her head and laughed. "Ah, forget it. I'm here to have fun. I'm going to have a little flutter as well."

Paudie laughed. "Easy with the moolah, girl. Horses are a dangerous drug."

Megan put her entrance ticket into her handbag. "Do you never bet?"

"I might put a tenner or so on a good horse, but that's about it. I'm going to put a little bit on Diana's horse."

"Does she train horses as well?"

"No. This isn't a horse she owns, it's one she bred and sold on. It's owned by a syndicate, I think. But she's always very attached to the horses she's bred."

They made their way through the crowd. Paudie held Megan's elbow in a tight grip as they walked towards the stands. He was greeted now and then by claps on his back and shouts of 'Howerya, Paudie', but they didn't stop to talk. "We'd better make sure we get seats, or we'll have to stand, and then you won't see a thing," he said.

They passed bookies setting up their places. "Shouldn't we place our bets now?" Megan asked.

"Yes, we will. But I have my favourite. These guys don't offer the best odds. My friend, Bobby, is my man."

They stopped in front of a board that showed the horses running in the next race. A tiny man in a checked jacket and deerstalker hat was shouting into the crowd and making odd gestures. Paudie touched his shoulder. "Hello, Bobby, how are things?"

He turned around. "Paudie, my friend! And with a lovely lady as usual. He grabbed Megan's hand and kissed it. "An honour to meet you, my dear."

Megan giggled. "Hello. What a lovely day."

"All the lovelier now that I've met you, my fair lady." He winked at Paudie. "This is a grand girl. Hold on to her."

Paudie laughed. "Enough of your blather, Bobby, or she'll get a swelled head." He pulled two twenty-euro bills out of the pocket of his shirt. "Forty on the nose of Bare Necessities."

Bobby clutched his heart "Forty? My God, Paudie, you're going mad today. That's a complete outsider."

"I know," Paudie said. "But a friend of mine bred it. I'm only betting on it to bring it luck."

"You could do that for a little less, but okay, you're the boss." He took the money and handed Paudie a ticket. He beamed at Megan. "And what about you, me darlin'? A tenner on a sure winner?"

Megan opened her bag and took out her wallet. "No. I'll put two hundred on Bare Necessities."

There was a stunned silence. Bobby shook his head. "On such an outsider? Well, the odds are great, so if he wins, you'll get four thousand. But the favourite's so strong. Your choice is a risky business, sweetheart."

Paudie shuffled his feet. "Megs, are you sure? I mean, it's a good horse but that amount of money..."

Megan nodded and proffered the bills to Bobby. "Yes. I'm sure. I know you think I'm mad, but I have this feeling."

Bobby sighed and took the notes. "There's no arguing with a woman when she has a 'feeling.'"

Megan took the ticket he handed her. "That's right."

Paudie touched Bobby's shoulder. "Don't look, but there's Garret Nolan coming your way," he muttered.

"Oh shit," Bobby said. "Not him. I know I should be delighted, but when a gambling addict comes to you only to get his throat cut again, then my job becomes such a pain."

Paudie nodded. "Yes, but what can you do? If he doesn't go to you, he'll go somewhere else."

Megan stole a look at the older man walking towards them. Leaning slightly on a walking stick, he was tall and good-looking, with a shock of white hair and broad shoulders. Dressed in a tweed jacket and matching hat, there was a dapper, jaunty air about him, like someone enjoying a day out. But there was also something familiar about him. With a sudden shock of recognition, she realised who he was. "Dan's dad," she mumbled. "They're so alike."

"That's right." Paudie pulled her away. "Not a man I want to speak to right now. Or ever."

"But," Megan protested as they rushed through the crowd. "Why don't you want to speak to him?"

Paudie climbed the steps to the top of the stands. "Look, I see seats up there. Perfect. We'll get a good view of the whole thing."

Megan was quite out of breath when they reached the seats. She had to wait for a moment until she could speak again. "Come on, Paudie, tell me," she said, when they were sitting down. "What is it between you and the Nolans?"

Paudie adjusted his linen blazer and pulled at his shirt collar. "Oh, that's just some family stuff."

"Yes. So?"

He turned to look at Megan. "That family has always

behaved as if they were royalty. And if you must know, my mother was engaged to Garret in their youth. He jilted her at the altar. This turned out to be lucky for her because she then met my dad who was a much better man. She had a happier life as a result."

"And she had you."

Paudie nodded. "Yes. And my brother."

Megan stared at Paudie. "Your brother? You never told me you had a—"

Paudie looked into the distance. "It's a long story. But okay, I'll tell you." He turned to her. "My younger brother, Michael, and Dan were in the same class at school. When they were teenagers, they were always in trouble. Girls, drugs, booze, you name it. Mick was easily led, Dan a real leader, but very clever at not getting caught. Mick was always the one to get the blame, even though Dan was mostly the instigator. But hey, I don't blame Dan for Mick following him like a lovesick puppy. He was warned but never took heed."

"But didn't you try to stop him? Tell him Dan was no good?"

Paudie shrugged. "I did. But then I gave up when I saw it was no use. I was young myself. Only two years older than them and didn't really care that much. You know how you are at that age. Selfish. Mostly occupied with your own concerns."

Megan nodded. "Yes. I suppose. I didn't really connect with my family when I was in my late teens. My friends and school and boys were all I thought about. Home was just a place to eat and sleep."

"Exactly. And when you have to work on the farm in your spare time, all you want to do is get away and have as much fun as you can manage. Of course, Dan Nolan didn't have to do that. His dad was a solicitor with lots of money."

"Oh?" Megan said. "But I thought he was an estate agent?"

"He is now. Because he gave up the family firm for Dan to run. Land and property was a kind of hobby he got into when he retired. He did very well during the boom. Not so well now, I gather. Maybe that's why he likes to gamble."

"So what happened?" Megan asked. "I've a feeling something really bad is coming."

"You're right." There was a bitter twist to Paudie's mouth. "All this fooling around eventually led to big trouble. It was the drugs. Mick got hooked big time. Was in and out of rehab several times. But Danny boy kept out of trouble."

"Then what happened?"

Paudie looked around as more people arrived. Leaning closer, he lowered his voice. "They were in this gang, you see, and Dan was the ring leader. Anyway, to cut a long story short, the whole thing blew up one night when they were all in a car going home from a party. All high on coke. They drove like mad on the road up to the Connor pass. No one knows what they were planning to do there. But on the way down, they drove the car straight into a wall. One of the boys was killed, and Mick got the blame."

"Oh no!"

Paudie nodded. "Mick told me Dan was actually driving, but managed to put the blame on him. Don't know if that's true though. But I have my suspicions."

"What happened to Mick?"

"He got seven years for manslaughter."

Shocked, Megan stared at Paudie. "Where is he now?"

"After getting out of jail, he went to England. He got a job at a building site in Birmingham. He still lives there. Can't come back here, of course."

"Oh God. I had no idea. But Dan—"

"Is the model of good behaviour now, of course."

Megan put a hand on his arm. "What a horrible thing to happen. It must have been so hard for your family."

"Yes, it was. My mother had a stroke shortly afterwards.

She never recovered and died a year later."

"Oh God," Megan said. "How awful. I'm so sorry."

Paudie put his hand on hers. "Thank you."

A fanfare interrupted them. "The pageant has started," Paudie said. "Let's forget about all of this and enjoy ourselves."

Megan stared at the row of vintage cars coming into view, and at the newly crowned Rose of Tralee waving to the crowd. She tried to forget about what she had just heard, but Paudie's story was still in her mind. Not a very unusual story and something that happened far away in someone's youth, but she knew it would make her look at Dan in a slightly different way.

* * *

By the time the main steeplechase was about to start, Megan had nearly forgotten about Garret Nolan and the family feud. She borrowed Paudie's racing binoculars and inspected the horses as they went into the starting gates. Many of them shied and backed away and had to be guided in. But Diana's Bare Necessities sauntered in as if he was eager to get going.

"He's quite small," Megan said. "That's him there, isn't it? The little grey horse with the jockey in bright pink?"

Paudie took the binoculars and had a look at the horse. "Yes. I don't think he has much of a chance. The going is good. But look at the favourite."

Megan reached for the binoculars again. The favourite, number three, was a big bay with wild eyes. "Yes, probably. Don't know why I had that mad flutter. Just a feeling it was the right thing to do."

"You never know." Paudie patted her hand. "It's only money."

"Two hundred euros, what was I thinking? But if I win…" She trained the binocular on the little grey. "Come on, boy, you can do it," she whispered.

The crowd roared as the gates opened, and the horses catapulted onto the course. The favourite took the lead at once and was soon a few lengths ahead, with Bare Necessities trailing at the back.

Megan slumped in her seat and turned her head away. "I don't want to look."

Paudie didn't reply but took the binoculars from Megan and kept them clamped to his eyes. He suddenly made a strange noise. "What the—? Hey, Megan, look!"

"What? Our horse died?"

"No, he's—" Paudie pulled at Megan. "Will you look, for fuck's sake!"

Megan came to life at the same time as the crowd stood up as one and started to shout. She stared at the clump of horses and noticed that the jockey in bright pink and the little grey horse were nearly in the lead. The favourite was struggling, but the little grey soldiered on and, inch by inch, narrowed the gap. Then they were neck and neck.

"Come on!" Megan shouted. "You can do it!"

As if he could hear her, the little grey horse surged forward just before they reached the finish, and won by a head.

The crowd cheered. Paudie beamed. Megan threw her arms around him and burst into tears.

Paudie hugged her tight and laughed. "You won four thousand euros, girl. Why are you crying?"

Megan laughed and wiped the tears away. "I don't know. It was just so exciting. And winning felt so strange." She sighed and flopped onto her seat. "I can get some furniture now. Have the windows replaced. Finally get my house to look like a home."

"And I won eight hundred. What a star Diana is to breed such a little trooper. We must go and thank her. She'll be in the owner's tent in a minute. I bet she'll treat us to champagne."

They started to walk down the steps, the crowd milling around them. When they were nearly at the bottom, Megan noticed a commotion below. Someone seemed to have collapsed.

"Someone's been taken ill," Paudie said.

"Should we go and see if we can help?"

They were interrupted by a siren. An ambulance came into view, lights blazing. "There would have been one standing by for the jockeys," Paudie remarked. "Best place to have a heart attack, if you want the best care."

The ambulance stopped, and two paramedics jumped out. They immediately came to the victim's aid and applied an oxygen mask to his mouth. "Oh, good. He seems to be alive and breathing," Megan said, relieved.

They lifted the man onto a stretcher. Then Megan saw who he was: Garret Nolan, clutching a bunch of betting tickets.

* * *

"Something's come up," Dan said. He had walked into the house late one evening, just as Megan arrived home.

She put her bag on the kitchen table. "What's the matter?"

Dan pushed his fingers through his hair. "My dad's in hospital, and I've had to take over at his office as well."

"How is he?"

Dan sighed. "He had a heart attack two days ago. At the races."

"I know. I was there."

Dan looked up. "You were? At the races? What were you doing there? And why didn't you tell me?"

Megan switched on the kettle. "Do I have to tell you everything? Yes, I was at the races. With…" She paused. "I mean, to see a friend's horse run in one of the races. Then your dad collapsed practically in front of me. The ambulance was there in seconds, so he got help very quickly. I was told who he was by…" she paused again. "Some people who knew him."

Dan looked confused. "Oh. Who's your friend?"

"What? Oh, the one with the horse. Diana Connolly-Smith, my neighbour. Not her horse exactly, she just bred him. He won, actually." Megan drew breath.

"Did you bet on him?"

Megan beamed. "Yes. And I won. Four thousand euros. Isn't that amazing? I can afford to have the windows done now."

He looked at her blankly. "You won four thousand euros?"

"Yes. Couldn't believe it. It was like a dream. So exciting. But never mind about me. How's your dad now?"

Dan sat down at the table. "He'll be fine. It wasn't a major attack. But he'll have to be careful. Losing all that money didn't help though."

"I can imagine. Tea?"

"Yes, please. I could do with a cup. I'm a little stressed right now. What with my dad and then this problem with your house. So tea would be nice. Unless you have anything stronger."

"No." Oddly irritated at the way he made himself so familiar in her house, Megan busied herself with making tea. After she had put two mugs on the table and poured boiling water into the teapot, she sat down opposite Dan. "You said something's come up with the house. So what's the emergency, then?"

He looked suddenly uncomfortable. He cleared his throat noisily and started to speak very fast. "Well, it's about the deeds. The probate court made a mistake. We've found that the property is encumbered, and there's an outstanding debt of twenty-five thousand on it. It appears Pat borrowed some money a few years ago and didn't pay it back. That debt is now yours." Dan drew breath. "So…"

"So..?" Megan said. "How am I going to find that kind of money?"

Dan shrugged. "Unless you have it or take out a loan, you'll have to sell." He looked at her at last and smiled. "But you have that amazing offer, so you could sell up very quickly, pay the debt and still be rolling in it. So that's pretty cool, right"

Megan looked at Dan for a long time. "No, it isn't. I love this house. Having to sell it would break my heart. Why can't you see that?"

Dan squirmed. "What's the matter with you? Don't you see that hanging on to this shack is madness? That you could buy any little cottage out there on the Maharees and still have some cash left over?" He reached across the table and grabbed her hand. "We could be together there every weekend. And you'd be near to The Blue Door, so you'd get to work quickly. Think about it, Megan. You'd be living in a gorgeous spot and not have all the hassles of doing up this ugly—"

The chair toppled onto the tiles with a loud clatter as Megan shot up. "Ugly? You call my house ugly? I think it's a very beautiful house, actually. I know it's run down and in need of repairs. But…"

Dan walked around the table and put his arms around her. "I'm sorry, sweetheart. I didn't mean to say your house was ugly. It's just that it's going to take so much work and so much money to do it up. Seems too much for a girl." He kissed her cheek. "Okay, so I was jealous. I don't want you to spend so much time and effort on the house. I want to be with you as much as I can. I can't stop thinking about you when we're apart. You're the best thing that ever happened to me." He turned her around and kissed her mouth.

She sighed and let him, yet again, sooth her into submission.

* * *

Megan pulled in beside Paudie's gate only half noticing the strange car with Dublin number plates. *Maybe some tourist looking for directions. Funny how this road seems to attract them.* Paudie often joked that he would have to start charging for information or put up a little booth selling coffee and a map of the area.

Smiling to herself, Megan went around the back of the house. The kitchen door was open and Denis wandered out, wagging his tail. Megan patted his head and walked into the kitchen. She stopped halfway in and stared at the kitchen table. It was laid for dinner with tableware she had never seen before. Confused, she looked at the linen placemats, the silver cutlery, the crystal wineglasses and the jug with artfully arranged wildflowers.

The kitchen was tidy, the stove polished and the dresser cleared of the usual disarray. There was a smell of something delicious, full of garlic and herbs coming from the oven, and a stick of French bread lay across the front to warm. The room looked like a photo in Good Housekeeping. *Dinner for two in my country kitchen, or something*, Megan thought fleetingly, before the door to the living room flew open and a woman burst in.

She stopped dead and looked at Megan. "Oh. Hi. Sorry, but…" She was tall and slim with blond ringlets framing an angelic face, huge eyes and a pouty mouth. Dressed in a sky blue tee-shirt, long cotton skirt and sandals, she looked as if she was about to sing a hymn in some chapel in The Sound of Music.

Megan ran a hand through her windswept hair and felt suddenly unfresh, as if she needed to put on deodorant and brush her teeth. "Hi, I'm Megan," she said and held out her hand.

The woman looked confused. "Yes? What can I do for you?"

Megan let her hand drop. "You mean Paudie hasn't said anything about me?"

She shook her head. "Uh, no. But I only arrived this afternoon. Paudie is out doing some farming or something. He'll be here soon. I hope," she added with a laugh. "Or the coq au vin will be a disaster."

Megan managed a pale smile. "Well, that would be... disappointing." She cleared her suddenly dry throat. "In any case, like I said, I'm Megan. O'Farrell. I live down the road. I'm doing up an old house I inherited."

The woman smiled, showing a row of tiny white teeth. "I see. I thought you were a lost tourist. She held out her hand. "I'm Victoria. Bunny for short."

Only now did Megan notice her America accent. *Grace fucking Kelly*, she thought, at the same time trying to figure out how Victoria could become Bunny. "Hi," she said automatically and shook hands. "Nice to meet you."

Bunny nodded. "Very nice. I suppose you're wondering who the hell I am, right?" Without waiting for an answer, she continued. "Paudie and I were in a relationship a while back. It didn't work out, so I went back home again. But I had to come over to get a few things I left, like my paintings and so on. So here I am. And Paudie was so glad to see me and asked me to stay a while longer. So I'll be spending what's left of my vacation here." She smiled wistfully. "And who knows? We might find that romance isn't quite dead after all."

CHAPTER 13

"Shit. She's back," Beata said. They were walking on the beach after a long morning of washing up and making beds.

Megan looked at Beata. "Why does that bother you? I mean Paudie had broken up with her when you were with him."

"Yeah, but she was on his mind constantly. He couldn't stop talking about her. I suppose he was on the rebound when he met me, so I was just some kind of consolation prize. Or a way to prove to himself he could still do it. She's one of those ballbreakers, you know?"

Megan laughed. "She looks like an angel from one of those old paintings. I can't imagine she'd break anyone's balls. More like she'd burst into 'My Favourite Things' any minute."

"Yeah," Beata sighed. "But the fragile-looking ones are the worst. I bet she'll move back in now and pick up where she left off. Turning the house into an art gallery and Paudie into her lap dog."

"I can't see that happening."

Beata stopped and looked at Megan. "How do you feel about this? I mean you and Paudie are pretty close."

"We're just friends. Close friends, but that's all."

Beata peered at Megan. "Really? Just friends, huh?"

"Of course," Megan said. "Nothing more. But nothing

less either. If he's happy, so am I."

"Yeah, sure. I wouldn't have thought he could resist a hot woman like you."

"Hot?" Megan laughed. "Me? I might have been once. But look at me now." She glanced down at her less-than-clean jeans and wrinkly cotton shirt. "A long way from the stylist I used to be. I haven't had my hair cut in two months or had a facial or even done my nails, other than cutting them short. I seem to have done some kind of Cinderella in reverse this summer."

Beata started walking across the sand again. "You know, you're much more attractive now than you were when you arrived. Much less stuck up and snobby."

"What?" Megan pulled at Beata. "What did you say? Stuck up and snobby?"

Beata turned around. "Yes, you were. You looked at everyone and judged them for how they looked and what they wore. You even tried to restyle Boris, remember?"

Megan laughed. "Yeah, you're right. And he listened for a while. Even went and had his hair cut and bought that pink shirt in TK Maxx. I thought you'd have a heart attack when you saw him."

Beata giggled. "Yeah, the Ralph Lauren look lasted for about an hour. Then he said it was too good for everyday and never wore it again. And the hair grew out into the same old mop."

Megan sat down on the sand. "Let's take a break. The wind's getting up, and they've promised a storm later."

Beata joined her. "The first storm of the summer. Means we're getting into autumn."

"That's a little sad."

"Yes."

They both looked at the sea in silence for a few minutes. The wind increased in strength, but it was still warm.

"So how do you feel about Paudie and Saint Victoria,

then?" Beata asked.

"How do you mean?" Megan pulled up her knees and rested her chin on them. "I told you. We're just friends, so why should that change anything?"

"So, what are you going to do?"

"What do you mean? I'm not going to do anything."

Beata glanced at Megan with respect. "You're one smart bitch."

* * *

Megan pulled herself together and finished painting all the walls of the house. She decided to use some of the money she had won to buy furniture. She contacted the firm in Dingle for a quote to replace the window frames, and made an appointment with the bank manager in Tralee to negotiate a loan. Not that she had high hopes he would agree but she had to try. The loss of the unemployment benefits, although small, made her finances less than impressive, but she did have the income from Beata and what was left of her savings.

She had a fun day with Beata in Tralee trawling through furniture shops. They bought a bed with an iron bedhead, a white bedside cupboard and a matching wardrobe. A bookcase for the front room that had been the good room and would be turned into a study-cum-guestroom. Her remaining furniture was brought down to Kerry by hired transport and carted into the house by two burly Latvians. The red sofa looked as if it belonged in front of the fireplace, and the antique desk fit perfectly into the alcove in the new study. With the addition of two large Indian rugs they found in a second-hand shop, an expensive patchwork quilt Megan fell in love with in a design shop and assorted lamps and framed prints, the house was now a home.

When all the items were carted into the house by a surly Boris who had driven them home in Beata's battered van, Megan sank into the sofa with a sigh. "Finally."

Beata looked around the room. "This is really nice. I love the white walls. Makes the room so bright. The curtains we found will look good here. And with the rug and the two easy chairs we discovered in that second-hand shop, it'll be really comfortable and cosy. A room to cuddle up in front of the fire on a wet day."

"If I can get the chimney swept," Megan sighed.

"Boris will do that for you." Beata went into the hall. "Boris, when you've set up the bed, come down and have a cup of tea with us, willya'?"

"Okay, boss," Boris grunted from the bedroom.

"He seems a little bit cross," Megan remarked.

Beata sank down on the sofa beside Megan and stared into the fireplace. "Yeah. He's not in a good mood these days. Doesn't even want to hump me."

Megan giggled, despite Beata's downcast face. "I love your choice of expressions."

"Do you think he's going off me?"

Megan sobered up. "I wouldn't think so. If he did, wouldn't he just leave? Maybe there's something going on at home in Russia?"

"Hmm. Yes. Could be something Russian, all right. They're so fucking *moody* all the time. Very tiring."

"Unlike Poles, who are furious, scathingly critical or cool but friendly?"

"At least with us, what you see is what you get. We don't withdraw into ourselves and make other people worry."

"Very true. Or never let anyone know how you feel."

"Like Paudie?"

Megan nodded. "Yes. Like Paudie."

"Have you seen him lately?"

"No," Megan said. "But then, I haven't been anywhere

near the farm up there."

"I saw *her* going into that French cheese shop in Tralee," Beata said. "I bet he'll get indigestion eating all that fancy food. Being used to a diet of cold pizza and ham and bread, I mean."

Megan looked up as Boris came in carrying a tray with three steaming mugs and a jug of milk. "I made tea," he said. "You don't mind, Megan?"

Megan cleared a space on the little table on front of the sofa. "No, that's terrific."

Boris slurped some tea from his mug. "I just listened to radio in living room. There is news of your man's father."

Megan poured milk into her tea. "What man?"

"Your man," Boris said. "The man you go with."

"Do you mean Daniel Nolan?" Beata asked.

Boris nodded. "Yes. The lawyer. He was on radio."

"Really? I haven't seen him today," Megan said. "What did he say on the radio?"

Boris shook his head impatiently. "Not say, do. His father do."

Beata shot up from the sofa. "For God's sake, Boris, spit it out! What the hell was it about?"

Boris finished his tea with a loud slurp. "Okay. Don't get your knickers twisted, Beata. I will tell. The lawyer man, Mr Nolan's father has been put in prison."

* * *

He was right. Megan heard the whole story on the evening news. Garret Nolan had been arrested for fraud. It appeared he had taken money out of one of his clients' accounts as they paid the full asking price for a house in Tralee. A deposit of twenty thousand euros was supposed to have been paid to the vendors, but when they tried to withdraw the money, it was gone from the account. His son, a well-known solicitor, made no comment, and the trial was set for later in the year. Bail was set at two hundred and fifty euros.

Stunned, Megan switched off the radio. So that was it. Dan's dad was not only a gambling addict but also a thief. Stealing money from his clients to feed his habit, no doubt. Poor Dan, having to deal with this. She felt suddenly guilty about being so obsessed with her own problems, she hadn't listened to Dan. And guilty for letting whatever had happened in his wild youth affect her. That had nothing to do with her.

Megan picked up her phone to do what she usually did these days when she had a problem. Talk to Paudie. But no. She dropped the phone on the table. *That's not possible anymore. He wouldn't have the time to talk to me. Even if he wanted to. Which he probably wouldn't.*

She heard a jeep drive up outside, and her heart skipped a beat. *That must be him. Coming to check the cattle. Maybe I could have a chat with him after all.*

She rushed out the back door and around the corner of the house but stopped dead when she saw who it was. Diana with the horses.

* * *

The mare and foal were unloaded and Diana went back for the other two. When the horses were settled and grazing, the foals suckling from their mothers, Megan and Diana leaned on the fence and watched. The evening sun lent a golden glow to the air and the mild breeze stirred leaves and grasses. The horses swished their tails and twitched their ears at the flies.

Diana let out a long sigh. "Isn't this the best time of day? When all the chores are done. And you can stand here and listen to the sound of horses chomping and watch the foals feeding, and all is right with the world for one short second."

Megan put her arms on the fence. "Yes. A good moment."

Diana glanced at her. "You don't sound too happy. Something wrong?"

"Not really. Just some stuff."

Diana put her hand on Megan's arm. "We all have stuff. I won't intrude. But if you want an ear, I'll be happy to listen."

Megan smiled wanly. "Thanks. I think I'll just try to forget it all and move on."

Diana nodded. "Moving on is good. A hard thing to do but in time, we all get there."

"I know. Thanks."

Diana moved away. "I have to go. Nearly supper time and we have guests." She clapped a hand to her forehead. "Oh shit, I nearly forgot. We're having a party next week. End-of-summer garden party. Well, it's supposed to be in the garden, but it nearly always rains, so we end up in the house anyway. What was I saying... Oh, yes. We'd like you to come. Next Saturday."

"A party?" Megan said. "I had nearly forgotten what that was. Thank you."

"You want to come, I hope?"

"Of course. Sounds like fun."

"It will be. And do bring your date. That handsome solicitor, isn't that right?"

Megan nodded. "Yes. Dan. But he might have some family problems. I'll be there in any case. Thanks for inviting me."

Diana backed away. "Excellent. Everyone's coming. I've even invited that Polish girl and her Russian. They'll make the party less bourgeois."

Megan laughed. "You can count on it. Just don't offer Boris any vodka."

"We'll just serve champagne, and everyone will get deliciously sloshed."

"Perfect. I'll get sloshed too."

"We all will. Even Paudie's saintly fiancée.

CHAPTER 14

"Will you do me?" Beata asked when Megan arrived at the B and B the next morning.

"What do you mean?"

"Will you make me pretty?" Beata looked at Megan with desperation. "We've been invited to a posh party, and I need to look good."

"But you *are* pretty," Megan protested. "You just need to…" She paused.

Beata nodded. "Yes. That's what I want you to help me with. The 'you just need to' part."

Megan stood in the hall and studied Beata. "Okay. But if I agree, will you do exactly what I say?"

Beata made an exasperated gesture. "YES. Anything. I'll even dye my hair green if you tell me it goes with my skin colour."

"I wouldn't do that exactly, but now that you mention it, maybe we could do something with that colour. It's a little—"

"Bleached?" Beata filled in. "I know. But it was a shade that was on a special sale. I think it's called 'champagne.'"

"Hmmm," Megan muttered. "That wasn't such a good deal. I think you could find something a bit softer. What's your natural colour?"

Beata shrugged. "Can't remember. Some kind of mousey brown. Or dish-water blonde. I don't want to go back to that."

"Oh, I wouldn't think you should. Something more like honey or dark ash blond. And ditch the orange tee-shirt and that pale green one too. And then your hair could be worn out, instead of tightening it with a wrench at the back of your head, and you should lose the black eyeliner and use a little blusher and lip gloss. And… do you ever wear a bra?" Megan flinched after her diatribe, waiting for the fallout.

Beata glanced at her chest. "A bra? But my boobs are tiny. Like two fried eggs. What would a bra do?"

"It could lift them a little. Make them rounder and give you a shape. You could even use chicken fillets to get them to look bigger."

Beata frowned. "Chicken fillets? In my bra?"

Megan laughed. "Not real ones. These are shaped like chicken fillets but made of silicone. You put them under your boobs in your bra to push them up. Gives a great shape."

"Oh. There's so much I need to learn. Sounds so complicated."

"It's not once you get the hang of it." Megan took a step back and studied Beata, her head cocked. "I think we can whip you into shape very easily. The raw material is great. Only one thing though…"

"Yes?"

"You need to quit smoking."

Beata rolled her eyes. "I knoooow. I will. One day. But not by next Saturday, so you can stop nagging right now."

"Okay. But after Saturday…"

"Yeah, yeah. Her eyes focused on Megan. "But what about you? What are you doing about the party?"

Megan smiled. "Me? I'm going to pull out all the stops."

* * *

'Doing' Beata proved quite a challenge. Megan had never had such an unwilling, protesting client. Not only did she balk at a change of hair colour, but she fought the underwear issue and every suggestion of party wear. Megan found herself standing outside a changing room in Tralee's biggest department store, bathed in sweat with a pounding headache, a stack of bras, knickers, tops, skirts and dresses weighing heavily in her arms. Beata was inside, struggling into a skirt and matching top, swearing under her breath.

"Have you got into it yet?" Megan hissed through the curtain. "How long does it take to get into a skirt, for God's sake?"

Beata pushed through the curtain and appeared, red faced, in a pink outfit. "Shit, I look like a marshmallow."

Megan burst out laughing. "Yes, you do. What was I thinking?"

"I want to look like Lady Gaga," Beata moaned. "Not the Sugar Plum Fairy."

Megan stared at Beata. She suddenly had a light-bulb moment so intense, it made her dizzy. "Of course! That's it! How stupid am I?"

"On a scale of one to ten, I'd say twenty-five," Beata said dryly.

"You're right. Shit. We've wasted a whole day. Take those terrible things off. We're out of here."

"Finally. Does this mean I don't have to go to the hairdresser's?"

"On the contrary, my dear. It means a long day at the hairdresser's."

"Fuck," Beata mumbled, retreating into the changing room.

"You'll be a hit at the party with that kind of language."

Beata stuck her head out. "You mean I have to change the

way I speak too?"

Megan pushed her back in. "That would be too much of a challenge. Go on, change. We have a lot to do."

While Beata changed, Megan put back the clothes she had picked, replacing them with just two items she knew would be perfect for Beata: a purple sleeveless angora top and a long black skirt. The complete opposite to the image she had envisaged. But this would not only work, it would be spectacular. Smiling to herself as she queued at the checkout, she bumped into someone. She took a step back. "Oh. I'm sorry."

"That's okay," the woman said. Then she smiled. "Megan! Hi."

Megan gave a start. "Oh. Hi… Bunny."

Bunny, who was paying for a cream linen jacket, glanced at the clothes on Megan's arm. "Nice colours. But not what I thought you'd wear."

Megan shook her hair back with a toss of her head. "I sometimes step out of the box. You should try it. Very liberating."

"I just came to buy something for a garden party we've been invited to. So linen seemed the best bet."

Megan eyed the jacket. "Perfect. Will go nicely with the roses."

Bunny gave the shop assistant her credit card. "Please put the jacket in the same bag as the shirt and tie I bought earlier."

Megan bit her lip. "Shirt and tie?" She couldn't help asking. "For Paudie?"

"Yes." Bunny took the bag the assistant handed her with her receipt. "About time he got something dressy."

"Oh, absolutely. He'll look very elegant at the garden party." Megan bit her lip harder, so she wouldn't laugh out loud.

Bunny looked at her curiously. "It's not really for the

party. It's for our weekend in Killarney. We're staying at the Great Southern. A romantic weekend. To celebrate a rather important event."

* * *

When Beata's makeover was finished, Megan turned her attention to herself. On the afternoon of the party, she dug deep into the last suitcase she hadn't unpacked yet. The one with her designer clothes she had intended to give to a charity shop, thinking she would never wear any of the cocktail dresses, designer jackets or tailored trousers. Nor did she think she would ever sashay into a room full of glamorous people in any of the Jimmy Choos, Louboutin or Prada stilettos. She was pleased she hadn't got around to giving them away.

Spilling the array of beautiful clothes, shoes and scarves on her bed, she studied the pile critically, picking the items up one, by one, examining each one, holding it up against herself and studying the effect in the old cheval mirror. Nothing seemed to be quite right. Item after item was discarded and thrown in disgust on the floor, until there was only one thing left on the bed: a slate-grey, sleeveless linen shift she had never worn.

Megan picked up the dress. It was a Vera Wang original she had been able to buy at a discount after a photo shoot at the department store. She had never worn it, thinking it was too boringly simple. But now, she found herself admiring the cut and colour and the clean, unfussy design. She slipped on the dress, picked up a pair of red Italian stilettos and put them on. She held up her hair and studied herself in the mirror, realising in a flash exactly what would make it spectacular.

* * *

The long tree-lined avenue led to a large, ivy clad Victorian manor house with a porch supported by pillars. The drive in front was already bustling with guests piling out of cars and jeeps. The gravel crunched as they all walked up to the front steps, where Diana, in a red dress, stood beside a tall, bald man.

Megan waited behind a blond man in a leather bomber jacket. She had spotted him earlier as he arrived in a red Ferrari and thought he looked too glamorous to be a local.

"Alex!" Diana squealed and threw her arms around him. "You made it. Oh, I'm so happy to see you. Where did you get that car?"

"I stole it."

"You idiot." She squeezed him harder, peeped over his shoulder and discovered Megan. She pulled away. "Alex, meet Megan, my neighbour. You look impossibly beautiful tonight, by the way."

The man turned around and directed his luminous grey eyes at Megan. He took her hand and shook it. "Hi, beautiful creature. I'm Diana's brother. That's a gorgeous dress. Vera Wang?"

Megan smiled. "Yes. How clever of you. Are you in the fashion business?"

"Yes, you could say that. I'm a photographer."

"Alex lives in New York," Diana filled in. "He's only the best-known fashion photographer in the US. Vogue, Vanity Fair, Harper's Bazaar…"

"Oh, come on, Sis, stop it or you'll make me blush." Alex winked at Megan. "Diana tends to gush." His eyes homed in on her neck. "That's a stunning piece of jewellery."

Megan touched the gold filigree necklace studded with amethyst, topaz and rose quartz. She had cleaned it with soap and hot water and polished it with a soft cloth until the gold gleamed and the stones sparkled. Putting it on, she saw it had a calm beauty that matched her dress perfectly and made her eyes an even deeper brown. "Thank you," she said. "It's very old. A family piece."

"Gorgeous," Alex said.

The tall bald man had noticed them. "Hello, Megan," he said, shaking her hand. "I'm Jack, Diana's husband. That's how I'm known, even though my family has been here for generations."

Megan looked into his twinkly blue eyes surrounded by a myriad of laughter lines and liked him instantly. "Hello. Thank you for inviting me."

Jack winked. "None of my doing, m'dear. But if I'd met you before…"

Diana pushed at him. "Stop flirting, Jack, you have work to do."

Alex looked behind them at more guests piling out of cars. "Maybe we should go inside? We're blocking the welcome wagon here."

"Yes," Diana agreed. "Take Megan inside and get her a drink, Alex."

They were interrupted by a battered van labouring up the drive, its engine spluttering. "What's this?" a guest enquired behind Megan. "Has Diana invited members of the travelling community?"

"No," Megan said. "It's Beata."

"What's a Beata?" the woman asked.

Megan was saved from answering by the van coming to a screeching halt in front of the steps. Boris, in his pink Ralph Lauren shirt and pressed jeans, jumped out and ran to the passenger side. He wrenched the door open and helped Beata down onto the gravel.

There was a hush as she appeared.

"Wow," Alex muttered beside Megan.

Diana gasped. "She looks amazing."

Megan looked at Beata with pride. This was the best makeover job ever. Beata's hair had been cut into a short bob and dyed mahogany with lilac highlights. The purple angora sweater and long black skirt hugged her slim body, revealing small, rounded breasts, a tiny waist and trim hips. The gold platform wedges and one enormous silver earring in the shape of a cross studded with crystals were the final touch. The whole effect was startling. Beata could have sashayed down a catwalk in any big city and been a hit. Here, in the driveway of an Irish country house, she was a sensation.

Nobody moved or spoke. Then, Beata glided up the steps as if she had never done anything else and took Diana's hand. "Hiya. Great house. Sorry if we're a bit late, but Boris couldn't get his arse in gear. Men, huh? No fucking use except for you know what." She winked and gave Diana a little nudge with her elbow.

Diana blinked and burst out laughing. "You're right there, darling. You look absolutely incredible."

Beata touched her hair. "I know. Megan did it. She tried to turn me into a marshmallow, but then she had other ideas."

Megan rolled her eyes. "I don't know what I was thinking. But when Beata said Lady Gaga, I knew what to do."

Alex couldn't take his eyes off Beata. "The make-up," he murmured. "Who did those perfect smoky eyes?"

"Megan," Beata said.

"Brilliant," Diana said. "Megan, you're a true artist."

Alex nodded. "Don't know what she looked like before, but right now, she's a vision." He beamed at Megan. "If this is your work, I'd be very interested in getting to know you better."

"Take the girls inside and get them a drink," Diana said. We've given up on the garden-party idea, as the met office promised rain."

"Drink?" Boris brightened. "You have Vodka?"

"We have everything," Diana said. "Alex will look after

you. Be careful, though, he mixes some very strong drinks."

"We'll watch him," Megan said. "We won't let him get us too drunk." But when she saw Bunny walking up the avenue hand in hand with Paudie, she felt getting drunk would be a very good idea.

* * *

Megan managed to avoid Paudie and Bunny for a whole hour, while the big drawing room filled with guests. Alex was very attentive and plied her with drinks and food from the buffet in the dining room. "The usual Irish summer party food," he said, handing her a plate of cold salmon, potato salad and lettuce. "But, hey, what's wrong with that?"

"Nothing," Megan agreed, as she nibbled at a piece of French brie on a slice of baguette. "I love this kind of food. It's so summery."

"Even if the weather isn't." Alex glanced at the rain drumming against the tall windows. "I'm glad Jack lit the fire. Are you warm enough?"

"Yes," Megan said. "It's actually not that cold. And there are so many people here. It's getting quite stuffy."

"True. Let's go and eat in the study instead. We can talk there."

Megan got up from her uncomfortable seat on the edge of the sofa "Good idea."

"You might want to escape the attentions of that hot-looking man by the window," Alex said. "He's been watching you."

"Who?" Megan scanned the room and met Paudie's gaze as he pretended to listen to a big ruddy farmer beside him. Bunny, in cropped white trousers, beige linen jacket and long silver earrings, tugged at his arm. But he was looking at Megan. Their eyes locked for a second before Megan looked away. "Oh him. Just a friend," she said airily.

"And the needy-looking woman beside him?"

"His fiancée."

"Really? I don't see a ring."

"I'm sure that's just a question of time."

Alex studied her for a moment. "Just a friend, huh? There are red-hot vibes that tell a whole different story." He took her by the arm. "But listen, my darling, let's you and me get out of here and have a chat. Diana tells me you have the most divine place near the beach. With a gorgeous ruin and everything."

Megan sighed. "Yes. But I might have to give all that up if I don't find a way to earn some real money."

Alex grinned. "Maybe we can come up with something…"

CHAPTER 15

Megan walked home slowly. It had stopped raining, and the full moon shone so brightly, she didn't need any other light to guide her home. She had taken off her stilettos and walked barefoot on the rough tarmac, occasionally stepping into puddles. Her mind full of what Alex had said to her, she wondered if what he had suggested would really happen. While they were chatting, he had floated the idea of using her tower for fashion shoots. It sounded far-fetched but the more they talked, the more real the whole scheme appeared. There were certain hurdles that had to be tackled first, but if the first attempts were successful and the word got out, she would have a steady income and maybe even a business. The house would be secure, and she would be able to keep it. "Saved by fashion," she said to herself and laughed at the thought. Beata's makeover had set off these series of events. Alex had been all fired up, and they had discussed future plans. He was going back to New York in a few days but would call in to Megan the next day—or that very day, actually.

Megan reached her gate. She stopped there for a moment and listened to the waves rolling in on the beach. She looked up at the moon and the wide, diamond-studded belt of the Milky Way. The horses moved softly in the field. She could hear a tail swishing, a soft neighing. She was about to open the gate and go inside, but changed her mind. She put the shoes inside the fence and padded down the sandy path to the beach. The tide was in.

The soft breeze cooled her hot cheeks and brushed over her bare arms. Megan slipped out of her dress and underwear. Naked, except for her necklace, she waded into the waves and threw herself into the water with a little shriek. It was quite cold, but the water felt invigorating and bracing. Just what she needed after the long evening of eating, drinking and talking. And trying not to notice Paudie and Bunny feeding each other bits of dessert on the terrace and laughing softly in that annoying complicit way of lovers. At least Bunny laughed. Paudie just smiled back and let her do it.

Megan turned and floated. Her head back, the water cooled her scalp, cleansing and sharpening her brain. Looking up at the sky, she felt like howling at the moon, screaming out loud into the cold, uncaring universe. But she came to her senses. What's the use of shouting at the universe? Wading back to shore, she saw a strip of pink in the east. *Nearly morning. Time to get some sleep and then face another day.*

With her dress wrapped loosely around her, the light of the new day guided her home. Nearly at her door, she noticed a shadow move by the gate. She strained her eyes to see what it was. A fox? Then she saw him. Denis, Paudie's dog, slinking through the fence and trotting up the road. Denis, who never left Paudie's side. Was he here alone? Megan looked up the road but the shadows were still so deep, she couldn't tell if there was anyone there. She wrapped the dress tighter around her and went inside, forgetting the dog and everything else as she went upstairs, crawled under the covers and closed her eyes.

* * *

The gate creaked. Megan woke up. She rubbed her eyes and squinted at her watch. Nine o'clock.

Someone knocked.

"Okay!" she yelled. "I'll be down in a second."

"No panic, sweetie," a voice called back. "I'll walk around while you get ready."

Megan got out of bed and pulled on a shirt and a pair of jeans. Yawning, she went downstairs and put on coffee before she ventured into the back garden, where she found Alex by the fence talking to the big grey mare, her foal sniffing his hand.

He turned around. "Hi. Slept well?"

"Brilliantly. But not enough. Didn't get to bed until around four. I went for a swim before bed and then conked out."

"That was brave of you." Alex gave the mare a pat and waded through the long grass to the stream. "This is a great place. Wonderful setting." He sat down on the bank.

Megan joined him. "Sorry about the grass and the weeds. I haven't had time to do any gardening at all. It's become quite a wilderness."

"That doesn't matter. In fact it's great. An Irish wilderness. A ruin. That beach. It's unique, you know."

"Is it?" Hope rose in Megan's chest. "Can you use it?"

"Definitely." His eyes focused on her. "And you."

Megan laughed. "Stop it. I'm no model."

"No, but you could be a great contrast. The down-to-earth normal woman and the emaciated, exotic creatures that invaded her space. Or something like that."

"Hmm, well, I'm normal enough, I suppose. With hips like these, ha."

"I think you're very attractive."

"Thank you. That's very kind."

Alex shook his head. "Can't believe you don't have men buzzing around you."

"Oh, I do. Or one man anyway. Who seems very absent these days. I have that effect on men."

Alex laughed. "I don't believe that for a second." He hauled his phone out of his pocket. "I'm going to call New York and tell them about my plans."

Megan got up. "And I'll make breakfast. The coffee's made."

"Great. I'll just have a look at the tower, and then I'll join you."

During breakfast on the back step, Megan wondered why she felt so secure with Alex. He didn't make a pass at her and his compliments were sincere, but more like observations than flattery. When he smiled and touched her, it felt more like the touch of a—then it hit her. She beamed at him.

He looked back. "Why suddenly so happy?"

"Because I've just realised you're gay."

He smiled shyly. "Yes, you're right. But why is this such a delightful discovery to you?"

"Because I like you, and now we can be friends without all that other stuff."

He nodded. "Very true. I have no designs on your body or you on mine. So... back to business now that we've cleared up our sexual preferences. I spoke to my partner in New York. He wants to come over here and have a look. Then, if he likes the venue, I think we'll have some kind of deal."

"If," Megan said. "That's not a word I like."

"Oh, he'll say yes. I like it and so will he."

"Deal," Megan said, "what kind of deal are we talking?"

"It's a little complicated, but this is what I have in mind...." Alex pulled a piece of paper out of his breast pocket and handed it to Megan. "It involves you as well."

Megan looked at the figures. Then she looked at Alex. "Is this for real?"

He nodded. "It's not a joke, hon."

"But it must be a dream," she said.

* * *

"Great news, sweetie," Megan told Dan on the phone that evening.

"What's that?" Dan enquired.

"I think I've found a solution to my financial problem. I'll be able to pay that debt if this works out."

"If what works out? Don't talk in riddles. Tell me what's going on, okay?"

"Sorry." Megan frowned. Dan sounded irritated. Maybe it was the problems with his father that made him so tetchy? "Too long to explain on the phone but the gist of it is that I met someone last night who made me a business proposition. I might be able to let the tower and the house, too, for photo shoots. Could bring in a lot of money."

"Sounds a little far-fetched to me."

"It'll work. I know it will."

"When pigs fly, right?"

"No, it's not—"

But Dan had hung up.

* * *

"It's absolutely amazing," Megan said to Beata, when they were making beds the next morning. "It's not all ironed out yet, but if this works, I'll have some kind of business. I can rent out my place for fashion shoots and hire myself out as stylist and maybe even make-up artist. Alex says he'll recommend me in the fashion world in the US and help me set up a website. Then I can do this on a permanent basis. Hiring out the tower and the house would bring in a lot. I might even do it for wedding photos too, he says."

Beata ripped a sheet off a bed. "Which means you'll no longer work here, I suppose."

"Yes. It might. I won't need to. And I'll be busy organising bookings and promotions. I might even do a make-up course so I can do all the styling for the shoots." A sheet clutched to her chest, Megan slumped on the bed. "I can't believe this is happening. I'll be able to pay that old debt and keep my house." She looked up at Beata. "This is all thanks to you, of course."

"Me? Why?"

"Because you asked me to 'do' you. And then I did that amazing makeover and you came to the party, and Alex saw you and thought it was so great." Megan drew breath. "What an amazing chain of events."

Beata folded her sheet, looking at Megan. "So, I was your advertisement?" She craned her neck to look at herself in the mirror and patted the gleaming mahogany bob. "I can't stop looking at myself."

"The hair's still great. And I'm glad you've changed your colour scheme to go with it."

Beata sighed. "Yes. That's all good. I wish everything else was."

"What's wrong?"

"Boris."

" Oh God, what's he up to now?"

"He's disappeared."

"What? Disappeared? What do you mean?"

Beata snapped her fingers. "Poof. Just like that. Gone. The day after the party. I noticed his clothes were gone and his bag and all his other stuff. Even the old leather-bound volumes of the works of Maxim Gorky he used to sob into when he was feeling homesick."

"Did he leave a note?"

Beata shrugged. "No. I suppose he had enough of me and my bad temper." She looked at Megan with despair. "I hope he's okay, though."

"I'm sure he is. He'll probably be in touch soon."

"I hope so," Beata sighed. "But I'm not holding my breath."

* * *

But he didn't get in touch. There was no sign of him anywhere.

With Boris gone and the B and B going through an end-of-season boom, Megan and Beata worked flat out the following week. They tried to report Boris as a missing person, but the police refused to have anything to do with it. As Boris was an adult with no health or psychiatric problems, suddenly leaving was not considered a reason to list him as missing. Beata was worried sick, but there was nothing much to do except hope he would come back or at least send Beata a message.

Alex kept in touch from New York by e-mail and Facebook messages. Things were looking good. His partner loved the idea and the photos Alex had taken. Megan discussed the whole thing with Diana one evening, when she came to check on the mares.

Diana beamed at Megan over a cup of tea in the kitchen. "This is a brilliant idea. Now you can pay the debt and tell that developer to get lost."

"I already did. Not the debt but the developer. I told him yesterday. He said it was a very bad idea, and that my scheme wouldn't work in the long run. But I have to say a big thanks to you for introducing me to your brother."

"I knew you'd get on. Delighted he was able to help." Diana patted Megan on the arm. "Better times ahead, I feel."

"I hope so. I don't think I could take more problems. Maybe my luck is changing…"

* * *

It started to rain around nine o'clock. Megan sat by the fireplace with her laptop, writing a message to Alex and chatting to her friends in Dublin on Facebook. The darker evenings and cooler, wetter weather had made her miss her friends. Chatting with them online was not the same as seeing them in person, but it was better than nothing. Dan popped into her Facebook page from time to time too. As the darkness pressed against the windows, and the rain smattered outside, the little screen was alive with messages and jokes.

She had lit a small fire with sods of turf, and the smell mingled with the hot chocolate in her mug. There was no wind, and the rain drummed straight down on the roof, the sound making the room feel like a cosy little island in the midst of a wet, cold world outside. *Soon autumn*, Megan thought. *Hopefully we'll get some nice crisp weather for our fashion shoots*. Alex was already setting up the first one for two weeks later.

Suddenly sleepy, Megan decided to go to bed. She banked the fire, put up the fireguard, switched off the lights and went upstairs. After brushing her teeth, she slipped on her cotton nightgown and crawled under the duvet. Settling her head on her pillow, she thought sleepily of the chores ahead. Talking to the bank manager again to arrange a loan to pay the debt on the house. Now that she would have steady income, they might agree. Or, if they didn't, she could use up all her savings for the moment and then earn it back within six months or so, which would mean having to stay working with Beata for a while, as well as developing the website and promoting her new venture. *Hard work, but worth it in the end*, she thought, drifting off to sleep.

What seemed only moments later, something woke her. What was that? A noise? She sat up and listened, her heart hammering. There it was again. A kind of groaning coming from the stairs… She reached out to switch on the light, but nothing happened. The power was off. It was freezing in the room, and the curtains swayed and billowed in the wind from the open window. A window she didn't remember opening. The sound increased in strength. Then the door handle turned, and the door creaked open.

Unable to move or utter a sound, Megan stared at the door. A dark shape appeared, a shadowy figure moved and swayed in front of her. Bathed in cold sweat, her heart beating, spiders of ice running up her spine and her breathing laboured, Megan's head swam. Finally, she was able to wring a sound from her tight throat, a kind of muffled, laboured scream. The figure stopped moving for an instant, then disappeared. All was quiet again. Megan sat up in bed, staring into the darkness. What was it? Who was there? She tried the switch again but the light didn't come on. There must be a power cut, she thought. She knew there was a torch somewhere but she was afraid to get out of bed in case it, or whoever was there, would appear again. But the dark shape seemed to have vanished into thin air. Megan jumped as the bedside light came on. The power was back. She got out of bed and grabbed her phone.

* * *

"A ghost?" Megan said to Paudie. "I don't know."

He handed her a steaming mug. "Here. Hot milk with a little whiskey."

She took it and drew her legs up under her on the sofa. "Thanks for coming. Sorry if I woke you up."

He sat down beside her. "I wasn't asleep."

"At two in the morning?"

"I'm not sleeping so well lately." He looked at her. "Are you sure it wasn't a dream?"

Megan sipped the hot milk. It had an added heat that warmed her stomach and calmed her frayed nerves. "Of course I'm sure. I know I didn't open the window before I went to sleep. It was raining, so I didn't want to leave it open."

"Maybe the wind blew it open."

"It's a sash window, so it can't blow open. And there wasn't much wind last night."

"Strange." He paused. "And there's no sign of a break-in or wet footprints down here. I had a look around, and there's nothing to suggest anyone was here other than you. Except the door was wide open. But you might have forgotten to lock it."

Megan shook her head. "No. Absolutely not. I always lock it. I've had the door fixed and a new lock fitted. I'm no chicken, but I'm very aware I'm on my own in this house with no neighbours."

"Right. Hmm. It is a mystery. Are you sure you didn't—"

Megan sat up. "No! I didn't imagine it or dream it. Someone, *something* was here, I tell you. The power went out too and then came back on again. If that's not spooky, I don't know what is."

Paudie pondered this for a moment. "Very odd, I have to admit. Do you want to come up to my house and stay the night?"

"With Bunny there? No thanks." Megan finished her milk and pulled the blanket tighter around her shoulders.

"Do you want me to stay?"

Their eyes met. Megan looked away. "N...no."

He put his hand on her leg. "Sure? Will you be able to sleep?"

"I'll stay down here. I feel safer, now that you lit the fire." Her body screamed with longing to ask him to stay, to cuddle up with her here on the sofa, or at least not take his hand—so warm through the blanket—off her leg.

He took his hand away. "Okay. If you're sure." He looked thoughtfully at her. "You know what? I'll leave Denis here with you. If anyone tries to get in, he'll give them hell."

"That'd be lovely. But won't you miss him? He never leaves your side."

"I think he'll be better off here for a few days. Bunny and he don't get on so well."

Megan patted the sofa cushion beside her. "Okay, Denis. Up you come. I could do with a warm, furry friend to cuddle up with."

Denis didn't need any further encouragement. He leapt onto the sofa and settled beside Megan with a contended groan.

Paudie laughed. "I was going to tell you not to spoil him, but I see that would be useless. I'll leave him here, then."

Megan put her arm around Denis. "Thanks. I feel better already. I hope he won't be homesick."

"With you spoiling him rotten? No chance. I'll be the sad one. We've never been apart, ever since he was a puppy." He got up. "Good night, then. Call me if there's any trouble."

"I will. I have my mobile right here."

Paudie nodded. "Good. I'll see you in the morning." He closed the door softly behind him.

Megan put her cheek against Denis' soft head. "Thanks for keeping me company. I hope your first time away from Paudie won't be too sad." Then she remembered. It wasn't the first time Denis was away from his master. Or—was it?

CHAPTER 16

The rest of the night was uneventful, and Megan woke up stiff but rested. Denis padded around behind her wherever she went, a reassuring presence in the house. She left him lying on a blanket in the kitchen when she went to work and told him she would be back at lunchtime to walk him.

"I should really get my own dog," Megan said to Beata later that day. "It's crazy not to have one when I live so isolated."

Beata nodded, absentmindedly rubbing a plate with a towel.

Megan took it away from her. "You've been drying that plate for ten minutes now."

"Oh? Yes. So I have." Beata sniffed.

"Still no word from Boris?"

Beata shrugged. "No."

Megan put her arm around Beata's shoulder. "I hate seeing you like this. I think I'd prefer you to be rip-roaring angry than morose and heartbroken."

Beata picked up a jug from the table and filled it with water. "I'm angry with myself. For being so hateful to live with that Boris had to run away."

Megan stacked the remaining plates on the shelf in the kitchen cupboard. "I don't think it was that. I don't understand him anymore than you do, but I bet there was a very good reason he left. And I bet he'll be back when you least expect it."

"I hope you're right. But you have other problems. That ghost or whatever it was. What if your house is haunted? Or that old tower?"

Megan laughed. "I'm not afraid of ghosts." She paused. "But I have to admit it was scary." She shook herself. "Won't happen again. Not with Denis there to protect me."

* * *

But it did happen that night. Not in the house but in the tower. And Denis was just as scared as Megan.

Denis suddenly gave a little 'woof'. Megan opened her eyes and stared into the darkness. "What's the matter, boy?"

Denis growled.

Megan put out her hand to switch on the light. But again, there was no power. Denis jumped up and growled again. Megan put her hand on his back. She felt the hair along his spine rise and his body go rigid. He started to bark.

Megan got out of bed and reached for her flashlight on the chest of drawers. She switched it on and pulled on her dressing gown. Denis was already running down the stairs, barking furiously. Megan followed, shining the torch around, finding nothing. Denis scratched at the back door and whimpered, followed by more barking.

Megan opened the door. Denis flew out, racing across the garden to the tower. Megan squinted through the gloom. Then she saw it. A faint glimmer through the slit high up in the ruined tower. There was a smell of smoke and then suddenly, flames shot out of the top of the tower, the jagged peaks outlined against an orange glow.

Holding her breath, Megan stared at the fire. Denis stood at the base of the tower, no longer barking but staring up just like Megan. He growled softly, then backed away until he was hiding behind her. Together they looked up at the flames that slowly flickered and died. A crow called out, making Megan jump. Then all was quiet.

Megan stood there, wrapping her dressing gown around her as tightly as she could and listened. She closed her eyes and tried to feel with all her senses the presence of someone or something. But there was nothing, just the smell of smoke, damp air and a chill that rose from the earth and clawed at her legs. She turned around and, with Denis trotting at her heels, went back to the house to call the fire brigade.

Inside, the power was back, and all the lights blazed. The TV was on, and the radio blared out loud music. Megan ran around and switched everything off, before calling the fire brigade.

* * *

"It was really weird," Megan told Dan as they walked on the beach. "A fire in the tower. High up. I think it was the crows' nests that were burning. The firemen said it was just a tiny fire that had gone out by the time they arrived. The electricity was off and then, when I came back in, it was on. All the lights had been switched on and even the TV and the radio. Who got into my house? And who started that fire? And why?"

Dan shook his head. "That's really eerie. It's happening again. Because of the—" he stopped.

"The what?"

"Oh. Nothing. Never mind."

Megan pulled at him. "Come on! If you know something, please tell me."

"Oh, it's just a story. A legend. Someone died in the tower hundreds of years ago. One of the O'Farrell chieftains. He was a very cruel man and used to amuse himself by seducing young women. You know. The 'droit de seigneur' and all that."

Megan stopped walking. "Really? He would ask young brides to come to the tower so he could ravish them? How awful."

Dan smirked. "Well, you know, in those days, they thought differently. Anyway, one of the women didn't take too kindly to this. So she came back the following night and set fire to the tower. O'Farrell died a horrible death. His screams could be heard all over the neighbourhood, so the legend goes."

Megan shuddered. "What a terrible way to die. But—" She stared at Dan. "Are you trying to tell me that this fire was some ghost doing it again?"

He pulled her close. "I don't mean to scare you. But yes, that's what I've heard. If something happens to desecrate the tower, the fire is lit and seen by the owner of the house. It happened once to your Uncle Pat when he tried to do up the cellar to use as storage."

Megan backed away. "So, you think using it as a backdrop in fashion photos might have angered the ghosts or spirits?"

Dan nodded. "Could be."

Megan laughed. "Oh, come on! I don't believe in that kind of thing. Don't tell me you do."

Dan shrugged. "I always keep an open mind. There are things going on in these parts that can't be explained." He took her in his arms again. "Hey, where have you been? Seems like years since we were together like this."

She tilted her head back and looked at him. He was so handsome, so sweet and alluring. His arms around her felt so good. She put her cheek against the rough wool of his sweater and breathed in the smell of the sea and his aftershave. "I seem to have been away from you for a while," she murmured. "But now I'm back."

He smiled that smile that always turned her heart to mush. "Welcome back, sweetheart." He kissed her deeply.

She closed her eyes and melted into his embrace. *Where is this going?* she heard a little voice ask. *I don't care,* she thought and pushed all her doubts away, kissing him back as hard as she could.

They sank onto the sand, tearing at each other's clothes, kissing, touching. Finally naked, not caring if anyone was watching, she pulled Dan on top of her. There was a new urgency in his thrusts, which excited her and she finally climaxed, screaming into the wind.

* * *

"So how are things?" Paudie asked on the phone later that night.

Lying on the sofa, Megan twirled one of Denis' ears. "So far no ghosts. Or fires."

"That's good. Last night was a little weird."

"Weird? It was spooky beyond belief. But the funny thing is, I went right back to sleep after the fire went out. And then, when I looked in the morning, there were just a few burnt twigs up there. The fire wasn't very big after all. But everything seems worse in the middle of the night."

"Could have been just a prank. Boys messing or something. You in bed?"

"No, we're in the living room. On the couch watching a movie. I lit the fire, locked the doors and made sure all the windows are closed." She felt calm and relaxed after the passion in the dunes earlier. Dan had been more than manly this time, as if the sudden urge in Megan turned him on more than ever. Afterwards, they lay there, laughing, talking, kissing, until Dan's phone rang, and he had to leave on urgent business. Megan put her clothes back on and walked home, where Denis greeted her with his usual enthusiasm.

"What movie?" Paudie asked, pulling Megan back to reality.

"Some Like it Hot. Denis loves it. He licks his lips every time Marilyn Monroe wiggles her hips."

"So do I. You remind me of her."

Megan sat up. "I do? But I'm not blonde."

"It's your hips. They kind of wiggle the same way."

Megan laughed. "Yeah, my hips are hard to ignore." She straightened up. "Hey, if you have time to talk, I'd like to ask you a question."

"Go ahead. Bunny's in the bath. It usually takes her hours. Don't know what she does there, but she lights candles and plays weird music and comes out all glowing."

"Oh." Megan found she wasn't interested in what Bunny did in the bath. Or afterwards. But she pushed the thought away. "Yes, well… Where was I? Yes, the ghostly thing."

"Yes? Have you come to any conclusion?"

Megan sank back on the sofa. "No. But I heard this story. About the ghost of the O'Farrell chieftain. Have you heard it?"

"You mean old Bluebeard? I just know he was a randy bastard."

"But not that he haunts this place? Or that there's a fire in the tower whenever the spirits think you're not treating it with respect."

"Where did you hear that rubbish?"

"D—I mean I just…"

"Dan Nolan, no doubt." Paudie jeered. "He has a great line in bullshit. Probably strung you a line to make you feel scared so you'd run to him for protection. Cheap trick, if you ask me."

Megan felt a surge of irritation. "Why are you always harping on about Dan? He's not as bad as you always make him out to be. I know he was bad in his youth, but he's changed. Everyone does."

"You don't know him like I do. You be careful with that crook and his family, girl. Don't let any of them fool you."

"I can take care of myself, thank you very much," Megan snapped.

"I'm sure you can. In that case, maybe I could have Denis back. I need him for herding, anyway. I'll be getting the sheep down from the mountains soon to check their feet and do the dipping."

"Dipping?"

"Yes, we dip the sheep regularly. Gets rid of parasites. Anyway, I'll be needing Denis for that." Paudie's voice was so cold it made Megan shiver.

"Fine. I'll bring him back in the morning."

"Make that the late afternoon. I won't be home until then."

"Okay." Megan paused. "So… that old legend. It's not true then?"

"It's a load of shite."

* * *

Megan switched on the washing machine and looked around the kitchen. "Is there anything else you want me to do before lunch?"

"No," Beata said. "I think we're okay. I don't need you until around four. Are you going back to your house to check on Denis?"

"No. I'm going out to Dan's friend's cottage. He said he was going there to get it ready for some people who are renting it from Monday. I'm going to surprise him with a picnic lunch."

"Some people don't like surprises," Beata remarked. "Are

you sure he does?"

"Of course. He'll be happy to see me." Megan smiled thinking about the great sex in the dunes. Dan had seemed unusually hot and bothered then. Was it because he thought someone might be watching? Or maybe Megan's need for comfort and protection had turned him on? "I got some deli stuff from the shop and those cupcakes he likes."

Beata nodded her approval. "Do you know the owner of that cottage?"

Megan picked up her purse. "No, never met him."

"Him?" Beata said. "It's not a him, it's a her. And a very cute one too."

* * *

The wind whipped Megan's hair into her eyes as she walked up the path to the cottage. She had parked her car at the harbour below, so Dan wouldn't hear her arrive. Carrying the cardboard box with the picnic, she padded up the front steps and peered in through the half-open door. About to step inside, she heard voices. Dan. Talking to a woman. Disappointed, Megan paused. It had to be his friend, the owner. She was about to step forward and introduce herself when she heard something that made her freeze.

"I need a little more time," Dan said. "If you could let me have the house the week after next, I'll make an extra effort to work on her. I'm sure our combined efforts will shift her."

"She seems pretty stubborn to me," the woman said.

"I think she'll come around soon. I thought she was about to. She was short of money. And then she couldn't draw the dole anymore, so that should have done it. The work on the house has taken a lot of her savings. I thought I had her when I told her about that debt. She seemed to buy it. But then she had to go and win that money at the races and that bastard from New York arrived with his offer of work and a whole new venture. Shit! I thought we had her."

"The slurry should have had an effect," the woman said. "I made sure they put the whole tank in that field. And I said it was a message from Paudie O'Shea."

Dan laughed. "You're a crafty one, Maria."

"What are friends for?"

"Oh, that was great, but my God, the ghost business was a stroke of genius."

Megan nearly dropped her box. She shrank back against the wall, nearly feeling her ears prick up. The ghost business? That woman had—?

The woman laughed. "Yeah. I'm quite proud of that myself."

"You enjoyed it," Dan said.

"Oh, yes, it was fun. I think I was quite clever. Especially switching the power off and back on again. She never noticed I had fiddled with the main switch on the board in the hall. Of course, it wouldn't have worked if you didn't still have a key to the house."

Megan felt sick. Standing there in the hall, she fought to breathe evenly and keep her legs from shaking. She wanted to leave, but a strange compulsion kept her there. She wanted to hear everything.

"Yes, but then she got that mutt," Dan said. "So that didn't work anymore. But the fire in the tower made me laugh. And then you running in to switch the power back on." He laughed out loud.

"Yeah," Maria chuckled. "She stood there in the dark, like an eejit, swinging her torch around. Even the dog was confused."

"But climbing up there wasn't easy. I couldn't light more than a tiny fire."

"It worked though," Maria giggled.

"Yeah." Dan suddenly sounded downcast. "It worked. I think she's ready for a little more."

"And then we'll go in for the kill. I'll think of something that'll drive her away for good. You might even save that English contractor a few thousand. He's getting a little impatient. Even though I promised I'd get him an extension to the planning permission through my contacts in the County Council. But it'll all go through in the end."

"I hope so." Dan sighed." But it'll be a while until I get enough money to get my dad off the hook."

"Don't look so sad," Maria soothed.

"Oh, how can I not?" Dan said. "The whole business is so hard for me."

"Oh, come here, sweetie," Maria mumbled.

Silence.

Megan peered through the half-open door. She could see Dan's back. Two hands sneaking up to his shoulders. They were hugging.

"Oh, Danny, I hate this," Maria said. "I hate that you have to flirt with that bitch just to get her out of the house."

"All for a good cause, though."

"You're not sleeping with her?"

Dan laughed. "Of course not. She's not my type. You know I don't like beefy women with big hips."

Megan had heard enough. Her knees shaking, she sneaked back down the steps to leave. But not before she heard Maria say, "Sweetheart, when all this is over, we'll take a long break together."

"Oh, yes," Dan said. "When we've sold that house and the land. Alistair is paying us quite a lot. Plus the commission for the sale. We could go somewhere really nice."

"Yes," Maria purred. "If I can get some time off from the dreary welfare office."

* * *

"Shit! Shit, shit, shit, shit," Megan sobbed, walking blindly to the harbour. "The fucking BASTAAAAAARD," she shouted into the wind that was now roaring into her face, so strong it drowned her screams. She marched to the end of the pier and flung the cardboard box with her carefully prepared little picnic into the heaving, black water. The box bobbed on the waves, releasing two cupcakes that floated, like two pink breasts, until the sea swallowed them.

Megan looked into the water and felt it pulling her down. It would be so easy... Such a neat ending. No more pain. She pulled back. No, not that. I can't. I have to fight. I have to show the bastard he's not going to win.

The burning pain in her chest was so bad she could hardly breathe. She staggered to her car and got in. She sat there, staring into space. Not thinking, just hurting, fighting to stay sane. Fighting to not go back and plunge a knife into Dan Nolan's chest. In her imagination she did just that and enjoyed the pain and terror in his eyes. The grimace of fear, his mouth open, his eyes staring. Oh, what pleasure to hear his screams for mercy...

She gripped the steering wheel, fighting to get her calm back, to stop the screaming in her head. *Revenge,* she thought. *I will get it. But not yet. As they say, it's a dish best served cold. Oh, yes. It will be cold. Like ice.*

She calmed down. Her brain began to function again. She knew what to do. She had a plan. Or the beginning of one, anyway.

CHAPTER 17

"O'Mahony Solicitors, how can I help you?"

"Could I speak to Jean O'Mahony, please? This is Megan O'Farrell."

"Megan! How are you?" the secretary said. "Jean just said she was wondering if she should give you a call."

"I'm fine. I have a little problem I was hoping Jean could help me with."

"Yes, of course. Hold on, I'll put you through."

Megan looked up as Paudie came into the kitchen. "Hi," she mouthed. "I came to bring Denis back. Just making a phone call."

He nodded and held up the kettle.

Megan smiled. "Yes, please," she whispered.

"Megan, hi," Jean O'Mahony's voice boomed on the phone. "How are things with you? Did you get the final divorce papers? I sent them—"

"Yes, thanks. Ages ago. And thanks for the support during that horrible time. Meant to tell you but—"

"Oh, that's all right. Glad everything worked out so well. Or as well as could be expected, anyway. So, what can we do for you today?"

"Well…" Megan hesitated. She looked at Paudie's broad back while he made tea. The mere sight of him gave her courage to go on. "It's about… I inherited a house a few months ago. In Kerry."

"You did? Jean chortled. "That's terrific. And great timing too. That two-faced bastard won't be able to get his hands on this asset. Where in Kerry?"

"Dingle peninsula. On Tralee bay. The house is right on the beach, practically. I'm there now, actually."

"That's a lovely part of the country," Jean said. "Wish I was there instead of a stuffy office in Dublin. But you didn't tell me. Did you need any legal assistance at all?"

"Not really." Megan smiled at Paudie as he slid a mug of tea across the table. "Not then, anyway. It was all very straightforward. The local solicitor took care of everything. But I've been thinking that I'd prefer you to keep the deeds for me and to handle anything concerning my property from now on."

"Of course." Jean paused. "Maybe you could get the solicitor in Kerry to send me the deeds? He should have the original in safe keeping."

Megan took a sip of her tea. "Actually, I have the original. He must have the copy."

"What? You have the original? They must have made a mistake. The solicitor always keeps the original. Safer that way."

Paudie said something.

"Just a sec, Jean." Megan put down the phone. "What?"

"I'm going out to do some fencing."

"Okay. Where's Bunny?"

"Gone into town."

"Right. Okay, I'll let myself out."

Paudie waved and left through the back door.

Megan picked up the phone again. "Sorry, Jean. I was talking to someone. Anyway, you were saying?"

"If you have the original, send it to me by registered mail, and I'll put it in our strong room for safe keeping. And then I'll write to the Kerry solicitor and ask him to give you the copy. Or you can ask him yourself when you tell him I'm handling your affairs from now on."

"Um, okay. I'll deal with him." Megan took a deep breath. "One more thing, though. I want you to find something out for me…"

* * *

"Trouble in paradise?" Paudie asked.

Megan jumped. "What? I thought you had gone."

"Forgot my working gloves." He picked them up from the dresser. "So… You okay?"

Megan took another sip of her now cold tea. "Yes, sure. Why?"

Paudie hesitated by the back door. "You're a little pale. And there's a look in your eyes." He shrugged. "Oh, never mind. None of my business. I just don't want to think that bastard Nolan isn't being nice to you."

Megan assumed an innocent air. "Of course he is. Why would you think—" She gestured at her phone. "Oh that. I just felt I should let my Dublin solicitors handle all my affairs. Being personally involved with one's solicitor isn't a good idea. A bit of housekeeping, really."

The phone rang again. It was Jean O'Mahony.

"That was quick," Megan said.

"Yes, took no time at all. And here's what you wanted to know—the planning permission expires in exactly one year's time. It's for a small caravan park and one building. Like a shop or restaurant. So anyone wanting to act on that should get going pretty soon. I doubt they'd get it renewed, as they're really tightening up on this sort of thing countrywide. But if you're a local, it's a different matter, of course. Or if you have connections. Those things are easy to fiddle if you know the right people."

"I see," Megan said. "And that old debt?"

"Doesn't exist. Your solicitor must have made a mistake. Or the probate office did. The property is unencumbered."

"Thought so."

"So, what are you going to do? I mean, it looks like a pretty hot property to me. A house in that location with land around it. You'd get a good price right now. You might want to think about this."

"Oh, I don't have to think. I know exactly what I'm going to do."

"Now, that's what I like to see," Paudie said when Megan hung up. "A look of determination and a cheery smile."

"Determination?" Megan said. "You bet."

* * *

"Hi." Megan smiled at Daniel's secretary.

The girl stopped chewing gum and her nail polish brush froze in the air. "Hi. Daniel's gone to a legal conference in Killarney."

"I know. I don't want to see him. I dropped in to ask if you could help me with something." Megan pulled a large envelope from her bag and started to speak very fast. "I have the deeds to my property here. I think you made a mistake and gave me the original. So I thought you must have put a copy in your safe instead."

The girl's face fell. She blew on her nails. "Oh. Right. But I'm not supposed to open the safe when Daniel isn't here."

"I'm sure he won't mind if you do it for *me*." Megan winked. "Lovely shade, by the way. What's it called?"

The girl glanced at her nails. "Pink Cloud." She got up and held out her hand. "I'll take that and put it in the safe."

"No. I'll go with you and make sure it's put in there safely. Sorry, I'm a bit of a control freak that way."

The girl laughed. "Okay. Come with me, then. The safe's in Daniel's office. We don't have a strong room like most solicitors. This office is too small."

They walked together into Daniel's office. The girl tapped in the code and opened the safe. She flicked through documents and envelopes until she found the one she wanted. "Here it is. Megan O'Farrell. It has some other stuff in it too, papers you signed about that will and your birth certificate."

"Oh, great." Megan paused, still holding her envelope. "Hey, listen, I'll take the whole lot and go through it. And I'll give it back to you when I have switched the deeds."

The girl looked uncertain. "Yeah, okay, if you sit out there with me while you do that."

"Brilliant. Then you can finish your nails at the same time."

It didn't take long to arrange the papers to Megan's satisfaction. Sitting on a visitor's chair, she pulled out the copy of the deeds out of Daniel's envelope. She glanced at the girl, but she was absorbed in her manicure. Megan replaced the copy with similar blank papers. She also took her birth certificate and put it with the others she was going to keep. Then she sealed the envelope and beamed at the secretary. "There! All done. Now you can put it all back."

The girl shook her hands in the air and blew on her nails again. "I'll put it in the safe right away. When I've checked the papers."

Megan handed her the envelope. "No need to open it. You'll only wreck your nails anyway." She stopped. "Oh, and just one more thing…"

"Yes?"

"Did you scan the deeds into your computer?"

The girl's face fell. "Oh God, no. I didn't. Dan told me to but I forgot. I'll do it later today."

Megan felt like laughing out loud but managed to hold it

in. She smiled at the girl. "Yes, you do that."

"I will. Thanks for reminding me. And, listen…"

Megan stopped on her way to the door. "Yes?"

"This is between you and me, right? No need to tell Dan about all of this, is there?"

Megan winked. "Of course not. No need at all."

* * *

The decision not to tell anyone about what was going on weighed on Megan's mind. Although tempted to share her predicament with Beata, she decided against it. Beata would be too biased and aggressive. Paudie hated Dan already and might have done something rash and spoiled the secret. She didn't know Diana well enough to confide in her. That left her with nobody at all which was difficult. But keeping her own counsel was probably the safest bet in the end.

She sent the deeds and all the other papers to Jean O'Mahony in Dublin, confident Dan's secretary wouldn't say a word about Megan's visit. The fact that Dan now had no records of the house, the will or anything else concerning her affairs was a huge relief. Now she was free to do whatever felt best and the support of the Dublin solicitor felt like a solid brick wall.

Despite her anger, she sometimes stopped to ponder about Dan. She found it hard to believe his plotting against her was driven only by money. There was something during that conversation with Maria that didn't ring quite true… Something he said and the tone in his voice. And that sad sigh. *It's his dad*, she told herself. *That must be very upsetting. He's probably hoping to pay the money back, save his father and clear the family name…*

Megan turned and twisted in bed. *I can't go on like this*, she thought. *I have to end it somehow.*

* * *

In bed with Daniel, Megan discovered hatred and revenge a powerful drive. She had thought she wouldn't be able to face him or stomach him to touch her after finding out about him. But, driven by this inner force, telling lies came easy and acting as if she wanted him even easier, as the desire for revenge burned constantly in her mind. She would pretend undying love for him if she needed, just to get to her ultimate goal.

"Ooh, yess," she moaned, meeting his thrusts with her own. "Right there, sweetie."

"You're amazing," Dan whispered.

She looked at his contorted face and closed her eyes. She imagined burning his hair, branding his chest with red-hot barbeque tongs and tying him up, sticking her mascara wand into his eyes repeatedly.

"Oh, yesss!" she screamed and woke up, drenched in sweat.

Phew. Just a dream. It didn't happen. I didn't have sex with him like that. How could I? She got up, wrapped a sheet around herself and walked to the open window to cool off in the breeze. She stared far out to sea and the white dot of a sail, just visible on the horizon. "Sailing away," she said to herself. "Away from all the hassle and pain…"

"What was that?" Dan said from the door. "What did you say?"

Megan whipped around. "What are you doing here at this hour?"

"I know it's very early." Dan put his arms around her from behind and kissed her shoulder. "But I came with some good news. What would you say if I told you the house in the Maharees is for sale? That you could buy it if you sold yours?"

She turned her head to look at him. "Really? But it would

go for a lot more than mine, wouldn't it? Such a unique spot. Especially if it goes to auction."

He wrapped his arms tighter around her and leaned his chin on her shoulder. "It won't. The owner won't put it on the market yet. So, if you came in with a good offer, the sale could go through without the cost and trouble of having to advertise."

"Oh..." Megan waited for what was to come. She could nearly read his mind.

She wasn't disappointed. "But, of course," Dan said, "the best thing for you would be to sell yours first. Then you'd be a cash buyer. Not many of those around these days."

"I suppose." She could nearly hear his next words before he said them.

"Yeah." He let her go and walked to the bed. He sat down and looked at her with that little smile she used to find so beguiling. "And..."

"Yes?"

"I have a surprise. You know that English contractor? The one who barged into your house?"

"Oh, yes. Alistair something. I still have his card somewhere."

"That's right. And you won't believe this. He came in with an offer this morning. Three hundred K."

Megan had enough. "Stop it right there, Dan."

He stared at her. "What?"

Megan took a deep breath. "I can't stand anymore of your lying and cheating. I've had enough of your charm and smarm. Enough of everything about you. So you can take those lovely eyes with the long eyelashes and the cute smile and the gorgeous body and get out of here and never come back."

His jaw dropped. "Excuse me?"

"You heard." Megan tightened the sheet around her as if that would help her stay upright. "I know everything. The slurry and the report to the dole office. The lie about the debt. The stupid haunting and the fire in the tower."

He blanched. With his mouth hanging open and a stupid look in his eyes, he wasn't even vaguely attractive. Megan wondered how he had ever seemed like the hunk she had imagined.

"Wwwhaa..?" he stammered.

"That's right. I know. About everything. Trying to get me to sell so you'd get your hands on it with your English partner. And your little romance with Maria Slattery. And all the rest," she added, not even knowing what 'all the rest' was, but she was sure there was more to it than she had just said.

"The rest?" he stammered. "You mean my dad and—"

"Yeah. That too," Megan snapped. "And Paudie's brother. What a lovely family you are."

Dan rubbed his face. "I don't understand what's going on here. If you know about my dad, then surely, you'd understand why I did what I did. Why I desperately need to make some money."

"Of course. But not that you had to go to such lengths to try and wreck my life. You used me, Dan. You lied and cheated, so you'd get your hands on my house."

"It wasn't like that," he started. "It was because—"

"Get out," Megan snarled.

He shot up from the bed. "Don't you stand there looking so self-righteous. You're no saint yourself. And you used me too."

"What? I used you? How?"

"For sex."

Megan burst out laughing. "Yeah, right. That's very funny, considering—"

"What?"

"I wasn't going to say anything but hey, why should I be kind to someone who's done what you did to me? I used you for sex?" She laughed again. "If I was going to use anyone for sex, don't you think I'd pick someone who was good at it? And someone with a little more than that shrimp you call a penis?"

He gasped. "But we... You enjoyed it. I made you come every time."

"No you didn't."

His eyes narrowed. "You faked it?"

Megan nodded. "Every time."

"You bitch."

"Ha, ha, yeah right. Coming from a shit like you, that's a compliment." Megan suddenly felt so sick of him she wanted to scream. "Get out of here, I said. Just go and don't ever contact me again."

He stood up very slowly, as if his legs were too weak to carry him. "I see. Okay, I'll go. I'll send you all your papers. I don't want you as a client if you have that kind of attitude."

"Ha, I already have them. Got them from that nitwit you call a receptionist the other day. I'd hire someone with a few more brain cells if I were you."

He shot her a withering glance, then turned and shuffled out the door, his shoulders slumped, his head bowed. He slammed the door shut and was gone.

Her knees shaking, Megan sat down. The feeling of victory only lasted a few seconds. Then she put her head in her hands and wept.

CHAPTER 18

"Models," Beata said on the phone ten days later. "They're such a pain. In fact all the fashion people are. Except Alex. He's a sweetie. But the rest are nothing but trouble."

The phone to her ear, Megan walked out the door toward the tower, where a tent had been erected for the photo shoot and all the paraphernalia that was needed. "What's the problem? I thought they said they would eat very little, so you wouldn't have to cook those big breakfasts for them."

"Oh, they have tiny breakfasts. But quinoa? And omelettes made out of egg whites? And two slices of apples and half a grapefruit... Shit, Megan, tiny breakfasts, but more trouble than a truckload of fried egg and bacon."

Megan giggled. "I see what you mean."

"And they all smoke like chimneys to keep themselves so skinny, and one of the girls wants boiled water with a slice of lemon before going to bed. Which is two in the morning." Beata sighed heavily.

"I know. It's hard work for you. But they'll spend the day here for the shoot. And if all goes well, they'll be gone by tomorrow."

"Why couldn't they stay with Diana?"

"I told you. Diana's children are home from their summer in Cape Cod and are staying with their parents before university starts in a couple of weeks. She has her hands full, with Alex and his partner staying there as well."

"Yeah, I know. I suppose I'll just have to put up with it. Great to get more guests now that there's a lull."

"And if this works, you'll have them regularly. So you might as well get used to it."

"Yeah, right. I'll have to get some more help though. There's still no sign of Boris, and you're busy with your new website, so…"

Megan felt a dart of guilt. "I'm sorry about that. I'll come and help out when the shoot is over."

"Don't worry. I'll survive." Beata hung up.

Megan was on her way to check the tent when she heard a car at the gate. She looked round the corner and discovered Paudie's jeep with a trailer full of bleating sheep. She gave a yelp of dismay and ran towards him.

"Hey! Don't unload the sheep. I have a photo shoot here, and we need the field to be empty. You can't use it until we're finished. I told you about this a few days ago."

Paudie glared at her from the driver's seat. "Yeah. So you did. But I forgot what days you said. I've finished dipping them, and now I need a field for them. I've nowhere else to put them, and the grass is still good."

"What about the paddock behind your house? Couldn't you keep them there for a while?"

Paudie drummed his fingers on the steering wheel. "No. Bunny doesn't like animals so near the house. Flies. And bad smells." He sighed.

"Oh. That's a bit unrealistic though, isn't it? I mean, in the country, that's what you get. Flies and smelly stuff. She'll get used to it in time. I did."

He turned his head and looked at her. "Yes. But she isn't like you. Not the least bit."

"I suppose not. Is she going back to America soon?"

"No. We're making plans."

"Plans?" Megan asked, puzzled by the flat tone on his

voice.

"Yes." Without another word, he got out of the jeep and walked to the trailer. "Look, I have no choice. "

"No," Megan said, pulling at his arm. "You can't. Please, Paudie, you know I have this contract with the fashion people. It's the very first shoot, and it has to be perfect, or they won't come back."

He stopped. "Why are Diana's horses allowed in the other field, then?"

Megan sighed. "Because they make a beautiful backdrop to the photos. I *told* you about that."

Paudie frowned. "Big deal. I have to earn a living here, can't you understand that? And these animals need feeding. The last few weeks of summer in good grass can save me a lot of hassle and money."

Megan backed away. His eyes were so cold, his voice so clipped and hostile. What happened to their friendship? The close contact they had all this summer? "Okay," she said. "I realise all that. But you have to understand that this is my land, and this contract with the fashion shoot is *my* way of earning a living, my chance to hang on to my house and keep the land with it."

They looked at each other in silence. Paudie's jaw tightened. Megan clenched and unclenched her fists.

She cleared her throat and put her hand on his arm again. "How about this—if the shoot goes as planned, they'll wrap up tonight. Then you can come back with the sheep and put them in the field."

Paudie looked at her hand on his arm. Then back at her. His eyes were veiled, but she thought she saw resentment there. "Right. Call me to give me the all clear." He jumped into the driver's seat, started up the jeep and backed into the road.

* * *

The photo shoot went as planned. The sun came out as if on cue. A light breeze played with the models' hair and made the summer dresses flow around their long limbs exactly the way Alex wanted. The horses grazed and flicked their tails, positioning themselves without prompting just so for the perfect composition. Alex beamed, his assistant giggled and the whole cast exuded contentment.

The perfection continued on the beach for the swimwear shots, with a flat calm sea and waves washing up on the sand, lapping romantically at the girls' bare feet. They had to shoot in long focus to hide the models' goosebumps in the chill of the late afternoon, but even that turned out perfectly, with just the right golden light and blue skies.

Alex smiled at Megan as he packed his cameras in the tent. "Absolutely amazing, darling. Couldn't have been more perfect if we said a million prayers to the gods of fashion."

Megan sighed and stretched. "I'm exhausted. Never knew doing make-up on three models would be so tiring. But there were so many different outfits to match and so many different looks. And I'm a bit rusty. Styles have changed since last summer. Make-up too."

"You did very well. I'm sure the pictures will be great. The light here's fantastic. We'll be back in late October for next year's fall and winter collections. And I might even manage to do some advertising in the meantime. This is a unique place both for scenery and light."

"When it's not raining."

Alex smiled and shrugged. "I know. But if you check the weather forecast you can usually hit a good few hours."

"If you're lucky."

"Don't be so negative." He closed the case and took out his smartphone. "You did great with the make-up, but if you're interested in learning a bit more, I'll try to organise a two-month apprenticeship with one of the top make-up artists in New York."

"That'd be fantastic, Alex."

"And you could stay with Trevor and me in our apartment on the Upper East side."

"Sounds great." Megan stifled a yawn. "Sorry. I'm really tired."

"Hey, we're going to that quaint pub to celebrate. Why don't you come with us?"

Megan shook her head. "Thanks, but I'm exhausted. I'll just tidy up and have something to eat. Then I'll flop on the couch and read a book."

Alex looked up from his phone. "You seem a little sad. Is your boyfriend away?"

Megan folded one of the director's chairs and put it on top of the pile to go into Alex's rented Land Rover. "Boyfriend? I haven't got one. We broke up about two weeks ago. Just after the party."

"Oh. I'm sorry. Maybe he wasn't right for you?"

"No, he wasn't. I was fooled by a pretty face and some sweet talking. Never mind. I'm kind of over that now," Megan said, suddenly discovering she really was. This realisation gave her an immediate lift. "You know what? I really don't care. I just felt it right now, this moment when you asked me. I don't give a shit about Daniel Nolan." She hugged Alex. "This is so great! All thanks to you."

He laughed and hugged her back. "I'm happy for you. I hope you'll enjoy this new freedom."

"Freedom?" Megan mused. "Yes, that's what it is. Freedom from being hurt and taking it all to heart. I don't even think much about my ex-husband anymore or what he did to me." She looked thoughtfully at Alex. "It's the house and then this little business I feel is just starting. It's doing things for me without having to consider anyone else. You know what? I think I'll give singledom a go. Maybe I'll discover I'm 'the one'?"

"That will make you both strong and dangerous," Alex said.

Megan let go of Alex and took a step back. "Yes. I like that." She flexed her arm muscles. "I'm strong. And dangerous. There'll only be one person's terms from now on. Mine."

* * *

After calling Paudie to tell him the field was now available, Megan lit a fire and settled on the couch with a plate of pasta and a glass of wine. She stacked cushions behind her back and put her feet up. Finally a moment to herself.

She finished the pasta and poured another glass of wine. Staring into the fire, she went over the previous few weeks, sorting everything into the right order of importance and filing it away. She was truly over Dan and found she couldn't care less about what had happened. He had tried to use her, but she had won that particular battle. It had been painful, but as it was behind her, she felt no pain, no need for revenge. Time to move on. A new life and a new way of living. On her own terms. That was exciting, and it had happened by accident. It felt as if it was meant to be, waiting for her around the corner all this time.

Megan yawned and put the glass on the coffee table. Time to go to bed. But she stayed there, reluctant to leave the cosy spot, looking at the flickering flames in the grate, her mind far away.

The door opened. Megan looked up. Paudie. She yawned and stretched. "Hi. I'm nearly asleep. How did you get in?"

"The ghost of the O'Farrell chieftain let me in," he said with a flicker of a smile.

Megan laughed. "That silly story. Can't believe I fell for that even for a second."

"Maybe you hoped it was true? Your very own ghost."

"Yeah, that would have been fun. But come in. Have some wine. There are glasses in the cupboard over there."

He walked into the room, poured himself some wine and sat on the edge of the sofa, looking into the fire. "Funny how there are two things you can look at forever. A fire and waves rolling onto a beach."

"That's true. Sheep all settled in the field?"

"Yes. Thanks. Sorry about the aggro earlier. I'm a little stressed. Lots of things to consider. Plans, you know?"

Megan nodded. "I know. Plans are good, though. Changes are good. As long as everyone agrees and is happy."

Paudie sipped his wine. "That's the crux. Everyone has to be happy."

Startled by his morose look, Megan studied him for a moment. "So ... are you saying that the person *not* happy is you?"

He sighed deeply and turned his head to look at her. "I suppose I shouldn't bore you with this. But I've nobody else to talk to. And we're still friends, right?"

"Of course." Megan pulled her legs under her and patted the sofa cushions. "Come on, get comfortable. I'll listen."

Paudie sank back against the cushions. Staring into the fire, he told Megan the whole story. "Bunny and I... we kind of found each other again. We've had a great few weeks. Like a honeymoon. Bunny is such a homemaker. Cooks, cleans, organises. Makes the house into a very pretty place, a real show house. I liked that. I got used to a clean and tidy house and gourmet meals. And in bed, she's so—" He glanced at Megan. "Okay, let's skip that bit. Not that there's been a lot of that lately"

"I get the picture."

"Yeah. Well, all would be fine and dandy if it wasn't for this idea of Bunny's. Or, more than an idea, a real scheme." He frowned. "She wants to go into organic farming."

"But what's wrong with that?" Megan asked, confused. "Doesn't that mean just changing things around a little? Feeding the cattle organic stuff and not using antibiotics and—"

"It would if it involved cattle. But she wants to get rid of all the animals and grow things instead."

Megan was horrified. "What? Get rid of the cattle and sheep? But that's the love of your life. That's why you've stuck to farming all these years."

"That's true." He sighed and pushed his hand through his hair. "She says they're hard work. And they are. But hell, Megan, it's the animals I love the most. I don't care much for tillage or growing things. A farm without animals is a dead place."

"Of course it is." Megan thought of Paudie up in the mountains, checking his flock. So happy. So at one with animals and hills and fields. Was that going to disappear? The wild, mountainy man aspect of him she liked so much? "That's so much part of you, Paudie. Without it, you'd be—"

"What?"

"Emasculated," she whispered.

His gaze met hers. He put his hand on her knee and moved closer. "Yes. That's exactly how I feel. I knew you'd understand, Megs. You always do."

She put her hand over his. "Yes. Of course. You're my best friend. I've missed you, you know. But I didn't want to intrude—" She stopped when he moved closer still. What was that look in his eyes? Friendship? No, more than that. Much more.

When he leaned over and took her in his arms, she knew what was going to happen next. What she had been waiting for ever since he stepped into the room. "Oh, Paudie," she whispered, but was silenced by his mouth on hers in a kiss hotter than the fire flickering in the grate.

His tongue pushed gently into her eager mouth. She

responded with fervour and hunger, wanting more, pressing her body against his, her skin burning. His hands slipped from her shoulders to her breasts. Forgetting Dan, Bunny, the organic farming and all the other harassments, she moaned softly as his fingers played with her nipples through the thin fabric of her shirt. His warm lips moved down her neck to the little hollow where she liked to be kissed. How did he know? As he pressed her closer, she could feel he was aroused. A dart of fear shot into her muddled brain.

She broke away. "Please... No... I can't."

"Why not?" he whispered into her neck.

"Bunny. You and she are—"

"So over," he muttered. "What about you and Nolan, then?"

"That's over too," she mumbled into his chest.

"I heard he's moving to Dublin."

"Good riddance."

"Yeah." He started to unbutton her shirt. "Forget them. Forget everything."

"Okay," she murmured, feeling all her reservations and fears floating away through the half-open window into the black, still night. His rough, calloused hands were gentle on her skin, his lips soft and velvety. He smelled of soap and something earthy and pungent which mingled into a heady mix she couldn't resist.

"Oh, yes, right there," she mumbled, as he instinctively found all her erogenous zones.

Before she could gather her wits, he had taken her shirt off and zipped open her jeans. A few seconds later, they were both naked, their clothes in a pile on the floor. How did he do it? she wondered. How could he strip her so easily and so expertly, touching her most sensitive spots as he went, flicking her nipples with his tongue, then cupping both her breasts in his hands before his slid them down her stomach to her groin, where his fingers did a little dance that excited her beyond control.

He pulled back and looked at her, his eyes scanning her body. "You're beautiful."

She blushed. Suddenly shy, she tried to shield herself with the blanket, but he pulled it away. "Don't be shy. I've seen you naked before."

She froze. "You have? When?"

"The morning after Diana's party. I saw you swimming. It was five o'clock in the morning, and the sun was just rising."

"You spied on me?"

Paudie laughed. "No. I'm not a peeping Tom. I was walking on the beach. Couldn't sleep. There was a bit of an argument, and then I needed to clear my head. So I took Denis and went for a stroll. I go down to the beach sometimes when I need to think. Or say a prayer. It's better than any church. God's creation instead of a building. And there you were, coming out of the waves like Venus. Naked. Wearing the old necklace. I don't think I've ever seen anyone so beautiful."

"Oh God. I saw Denis afterwards but thought nothing of it. I guessed he was out hunting rabbits or something. It was such a bright, beautiful morning and very warm."

He ran his hands over her hips, grasped her waist and kissed her chest. "I couldn't get you out of my mind since then." He lowered himself onto her body.

She closed her eyes as she felt his flat, hairy chest on hers and his erection push between her legs. She grasped his buttocks and arched herself against him. Unlike Dan, he was very well endowed, and she flinched for a moment, wondering how he would fit. But when he slid inside, he filled a void in both her body and heart. They fit together perfectly. It was amazing, she thought as they moved in sublime rhythm, so amazing she thought it was a dream.

But it was real. They came at the same time, something that had never happened to her before. His eyes looked into hers as the combined force of their climax exploded with stars and comets.

They breathed out in unison and smiled benignly, looking into each other's eyes. They didn't speak, didn't say the clichéd 'wow' or 'this was amazing', but exchanged a glance that said what words could not express.

Megan closed her eyes and drifted off. As if in a dream, she felt Paudie moving away and cover her with a blanket. She heard him tiptoe out of the room, but she was so tired she couldn't move or think. She knew he was leaving. She wanted to protest, call him back, tell him to stay but found she couldn't. She let sleep overtake her. What had happened was too much to take in, too much to worry about. Maybe it was a dream in some kind of twilight zone she had accidentally wandered into? *Paudie*, she thought, *who are you? What do you want with me?*

* * *

A sound yanked her out of the black hole of sleep she had fallen into. Dazed, she looked around, momentarily confused about where she was or what time it was. The light was still on, and the dying embers of the fire glowed in the grate. There was that sound again. Her phone.

Megan stretched out her arm and fished the phone from the table. She glanced at the caller ID. Beata. She pressed the button. "Hello?"

"Megan?" Beata said in a near sob. "Sorry to disturb you so late. But…"

"What's the matter?

"It's Boris," Beata wept. "He's—" She stopped. "I can't bear to talk about it. Please, Megan, will you come here?"

CHAPTER 19

Megan slowly gathered her wits. Beata's call had startled her out of the dreamlike state she had been in since Paudie left. She pulled the blanket up to her chin and thought about what had happened earlier. Looking around the room, she somehow expected it to be different, as if a fairy-tale creature had paid a brief visit and then disappeared in a puff of smoke. Then she remembered. She closed her eyes and let the tears come. *Paudie,* she thought. *What was that? Just a brief interlude? We had this amazing sex and then you just left. I never thought you'd do this to me.*

The pain was quickly replaced by the searing heat of anger. He was just like all of them. Took what he wanted and then left. *But I'm not going to let it destroy me. Not this time. He can just go to hell. They can all go to hell,* she thought. *All the fucking men on this planet.*

Stiff and sore, she got off the couch and walked slowly up the stairs to the bathroom. She stood in a hot shower for a long time, scrubbing herself clean, trying to wash away the pain and the shame she felt at having been used yet again.

Her phone rang again as she dried herself. She ran downstairs. *Paudie,* she thought, her heart lifting, *calling to say he loves me. That he's sorry he had to leave like that…*

But the missed call number was Beata's, followed by a text message saying "please come as soon as you can."

* * *

Megan drove to The Blue Door with a feeling of impending doom. What was going on? Had Boris been found injured, or worse—dead? She stopped the car in a shower of gravel, flung the door open and raced into the kitchen, where she found Beata at the table, looking at a small object in front of her.

She looked up as Megan arrived. "Oh, Megan!"

Breathless, Megan stared at Beata's red eyes. "What's the matter? What's happened?"

Beata started to cry. "It's Boris. She pointed at the thing before her. "He came with this…"

Megan's eyes focused on a small, blue velvet box. She reached out, opened it and gasped. "Oh my GOD! This is some rock!"

Beata nodded. "I know," she wept. "He came here tonight. Just barged into the kitchen while I was having supper. And then he—" She sobbed uncontrollably.

"What? He—what? Come on, tell me!"

"He… he… got on his knees and asked me to… to… marry him." Beata buried her face in her hands and kept weeping.

Dumbfounded, Megan stared at Beata. "And why is this such a tragedy? A man comes into the kitchen and presents you with this incredible diamond ring and asks you to marry him? Wouldn't that be any girl's dream?"

Beata lifted her tear streaked face. "It would if he wasn't a fucking—Russian!"

Her knees weak, Megan sank down on a chair beside Beata. "What's so wrong with that?"

"I'm Polish, Megan. Do you know what the Russians did to us? Invaded our country. Forced us into submission. Then we had to learn their language. They were unbelievably cruel. The Soviet regime was brutal. My dad had to leave the country because of his political activities. Many of my relatives—oh, I don't even want to think about it."

"But that was a long time ago, surely? I mean, Boris is too young to have—" Megan stopped. "Isn't it foolish to let history prevent you from loving someone? To let what happened years ago stop you from being happy?"

Beata sniffed. "I don't think you understand. We fought so long for independence in Poland. We've been invaded by so many all through history. And now, when we're finally a free, proud people, here I go falling in love with the enemy. It's difficult for you to understand that, I suppose."

"Hey," Megan said. "I'm Irish. We were invaded too, you know. Occupied for centuries. Our land taken. My ancestors were forced to learn English and forbidden to speak Irish or even have their own church."

Beata sighed. "Yeah, but that was even longer ago."

"A hundred years or so. That's not very long in history."

Beata glared at Megan. "Sure. But how would you feel about marrying an Englishman?"

"If I loved him, I wouldn't hesitate. And my family would be fine with that, even though my great grandfather and his brothers fought in the Civil War. Some of them had to run away to America. But we get on now. The British and Irish have no problem with each other anymore. The hatchet has truly been buried. It's all *history*, Beata" Megan drew breath. She was suddenly so tired she wanted to lie down on the floor and go to sleep.

Beata pondered for a moment. "Yes, but still…" She sighed deeply.

"How could he afford such a rock, by the way?" Megan asked, eyeing the ring. "It looks like a full carat of the best quality diamond. Must have cost at least six thousand euros."

"He worked all summer at the surfing school. Then he took off and got a job in a supermarket in Killarney, working overtime. He's been saving up for two years, he says. Ever since the first time we met."

"That's so sweet. Even you must admit that. But you haven't told me what happened. He proposed and then what?"

Beata sighed. "I wasn't very nice, I'm afraid. I shouted at him. Something rude—I don't remember exactly what. I was so shocked by what he did. And I've been mad at him ever since he just disappeared without a word. So he ran out and slammed the door. I bet he's in Mulligans right now getting drunk."

"What are you going to do?"

Beata shrugged. "Don't know. I wish things could be the same as before."

"Things never stay the same." Megan looked sternly at Beata. "Listen, you have a very rare thing here. A man willing to commit. A man who worked hard for years to give you a beautiful engagement ring. I know and you know that deep down you love him with all your heart. So he's Russian? So bloody what? You both live in Ireland and, I presume, want to stay here. You'll end up feeling more Irish than anyone." Feeling dizzy, Megan drew breath.

Beata stared at her. She opened her mouth to say something, but was interrupted by a loud knock on the back door and a voice, "Beata, there's been an accident out at Mulligans."

Beata shot off her chair and tore the door open to reveal a breathless young man, his eyes wild.

"What happened?" she shouted.

"It's Boris. He got into a bit of an argument outside the pub. There was some kind of scuffle, and then he fell backwards and hit his head on the pavement," the young man said. "He didn't get up, so we called an ambulance. He's on his way to hospital in Tralee. Looks bad, the paramedics said."

* * *

The Accident and Emergency ward at Tralee hospital was buzzing. Nurses and paramedics ran around trying to keep up with the demand on the ward. A large number of people with various injuries thronged the waiting room and corridors. Several trollies with seriously injured and ill patients waited outside the cubicles, where doctors in scrubs assessed and treated as many as they could in the shortest possible time.

Beata and Megan looked wildly around, trying to find Boris.

"We have to ask someone," Megan said. "If he arrived here in an ambulance, they must have registered him or something."

Beata squeezed Megan's arm. Her face was pale with a greenish tinge and her eyes bleak. "If he's dead, he'll be in the morgue."

"Don't be morbid. Come on, we'll ask that nurse at the reception desk." Megan pulled Beata along with her and pushed her way to the desk. "Hello," she said to the nurse who was shuffling papers around and talking on the phone at the same time. "We're looking for a man who must have arrived here in an ambulance about half an hour ago with head injuries."

The nurse held up a hand and kept talking into the phone. Megan waited. Beata shivered and whimpered.

The nurse hung up her phone and looked at them. "Name?"

"Megan O'Farrell."

"No," the nurse snapped, "the name of the patient."

"Boris," Beata said.

The nurse lifted an eyebrow. "And the last name?"

"Demidenko," Beata said.

The nurse shuffled some more papers until she found

what she was looking for. "Here's the list of the latest admittances." She scanned the list. "Murphy, O'Mara…Hmm. Oh, yes, here we are… Demidenko, Boris. Admitted about half an hour ago." She looked at them. "Are you family?"

"N… I mean yes. I'm his… partner," Beata said. "He has no real family in this country."

"Okay." The nurse consulted her piece of paper. "He hasn't been admitted to a ward yet, so he must be in one of the cubicles. He'll be there until we find a bed for him."

"Is he very bad?" Megan asked.

The nurse shrugged. "I can't tell you that. You'll have to ask a doctor. If you can find one," she added as Megan and Beata hurried away.

Beata and Megan went back to the cubicles trying to find Boris. But there was no sign of him.

"Where is he?" Beata sobbed. "Do you think he's dead and they've put him in the morgue? Oh, Megan this is all my fault. If I hadn't been so stupid this wouldn't have happened."

"Please, Beata, shut up. We'll find him." Megan flicked open a curtain only to find a woman with both her hands bandaged and a man looking helpless beside her. "Sorry," she said and closed the curtain.

They continued along the line of cubicles, opening curtains, apologising to injured people and their families. Two bad burns, one heart attack and three hip fractures later, they still hadn't found Boris. Beata finally looked so distressed Megan had to get her a chair and a cup of tea.

"He's dead, I tell you," Beata sobbed. "We have to go to the morgue."

"Please, Beata, stop saying that. Maybe he's been admitted to a ward? You can see for yourself how disorganised this place is. Nobody seems to know where anyone is." She held a cardboard mug of tepid tea to Beata's lips. "Come on, drink this. It'll help you feel better. I put plenty of sugar in it."

Beata took a few sips. "It's horrible. I need a cigarette."

"You stopped smoking two weeks ago."

"I know, but now I really need a fag."

"Beata!" a voice said.

They looked up. Megan's jaw dropped.

Beata gasped. "Boris!"

Megan couldn't believe it. There he was, looking pale and wan with a bandage stuck to the back of his head, holding on to the wall for support.

Beata shot up from her chair. "Boris, sweetheart, please sit down. What are you doing walking around with such an injury?"

He smiled weakly and touched the bandage. "Yes. I got hurt. Hit my head hard." He sank down on the chair. "But doctor say not too bad. Must rest and good in few days. Got paper for medicine, and then I go back here for check-up in one week."

"I can't believe they let you go," Megan said. "A blow to the head can be very dangerous."

Boris sat down on the chair Beata had vacated. "Russian head much harder than Irish head."

Beata put her hand on his shoulder. "We'll take you home. You need to get to bed."

"Don't we all," Megan said, as a wall of fatigue hit her so hard she nearly sank to the floor.

"Let's get going, then," Beata ordered, her usual vim and vigour back in her voice. "Megan, take his arm, and I'll take the other one."

A little unsteady, Boris stood up and put one arm around Beata's shoulder and the other one around Megan. "This way I like. Two pretty girls by my side." He looked down at Beata. "But what was that you called me?"

"I'm sorry I said those things," Beata sobbed. "Called you a fucking Russian bastard and… Oh God, I'm such a bitch."

"Yes, you are" Boris said. "But I don't mean those things.

You always call me that. But just now, you say… you call me—"

Beata looked confused. "What?" Then she blushed. "Oh, that. I said 'sweetheart.'"

"That's the one. You never call me that word before."

"I know. I never felt like it." Beata looked adoringly at Boris. "But now I do, you fucking Russian bastard."

Boris beamed. "I love you, Beata, my very own Polish bitch."

* * *

The happy conclusion of Boris' adventure ended back at The Blue Door with tea and a plateful of chocolate chip cookies. But the sight of Beata sitting on Boris' knee, kissing him between bites of cookie and slurps of tea, made Megan feel like an intruder. She excused herself and drove back to her house, bleary-eyed. It was now three in the morning. Too exhausted to get upstairs to bed, she simply crawled under the blanket on the couch.

Beata's happiness had made her own misery even more unbearable. *Everyone's happy except me*, she thought, tears spilling into her ears as she lay on the couch, staring at the ceiling. She closed her burning eyes, exhaustion finally taking over. She half noticed the breeze from the open window ruffling newspapers and blowing bits of papers onto the floor but was too tired to do anything about it. Sleep finally won over heartache, and she drifted off to sleep.

* * *

Megan threw herself into work. It was the only way to cope with the turmoil in her mind, and the memory of the night with Paudie. She had called him the following morning but only got his voicemail, so she left a message. He didn't reply. She sent him a text message asking him to call her back. He didn't. His silence was puzzling and hurtful but she couldn't bring herself to call him again.

He had whispered such sweet words to her. She knew he meant those words, had felt it as they made love, and seen it in his eyes, so tender in the soft lamplight. But he obviously felt his future would be better with Bunny than with her. Or he didn't have the courage to break up with Bunny. Or—Megan racked her brain for an answer but couldn't find it. Was Paudie such a coward he would rather live with a woman he didn't love just for the sake of convenience? She found that nearly impossible to believe.

Work saved her from sinking into depression: making beds at The Blue Door; organising the bookings; shopping for Beata, who was looking after Boris and making him rest as much as possible; setting up her website and a Facebook page for her business; scanning photos Alex had taken and trying to decide which ones would be the best advertisement for her photo-shoot hosting; surfing the Internet to learn about make-up trends and fashion so she could provide an online fashion and make-up advice service. All this took up enough time to make her too tired to think and exhausted enough to sleep reasonably well.

There was no sign of Paudie or Bunny. Megan knew he would be busy on the farm; or perhaps he was selling off his stock so they could start growing their organic products? He had said Bunny wanted to plant fruit trees, the autumn was the ideal time. She kept away from the hills above the house and went shopping in Tralee rather than the local supermarket.

The local news was full of Garret Nolan and the trial. He was finally sentenced to two years in prison. Megan heard on the grapevine that Dan was giving up his firm and moving to Dublin. She felt a huge sense of relief that the chances of bumping into him were now very small.

Three weeks passed, then four. Megan got an excited e-mail from Alex one morning, inviting her to join him for the ready-to-wear fashion week in Paris ten days later. "It would be a great way to get a crash course in the latest trends," he said. "Trevor and I are renting a little apartment on the Left Bank. You could stay with us if you want."

Megan jumped at this chance. "If I want?" she replied. "Try to stop me."

His reply arrived only minutes later. "So happy, darling. It will be huge fun. We'll mingle with the fashion crowd and network like mad. I'd like to get you some sponsorship for your site, too, if you offer advertising. And you could get some great bookings this way. Try to get your website looking fabulous by then."

Megan smiled, feeling something akin to happiness for the first time in weeks. *Yes,* she thought, *I need to get away for a bit. I haven't been out of Kerry since I arrived four months ago. And what a strange time it has been...*

Megan stretched and sighed, realising she had been sitting at her desk in the front room for hours. She got up and tidied her desk. She had been neglecting the housework lately. The whole house needed a good going-over. She took a brush and a few dusters and went around the house tidying up, dusting, getting rid of cobwebs.

The worst mess was in the living room, where piles of Sunday papers toppled onto the floor, the cushions on the couch were flat and rumpled and the fireplace full of ash and clinker. Megan realised she had been living in this mess for weeks without seeing it. She rolled up her sleeves and got stuck in.

It wasn't until she pushed the couch away from the fireplace that she found it. A crumpled piece of paper underneath, covered in dust. She blew the dust off it, smoothed it out and peered at what was written there. Her heart nearly stopped. It was a note from Paudie. A note he must have written before leaving that night. Holding her breath, her heart pounding, she read the scribbled message.

The handwriting was difficult to decipher. Megan held it up to the light. It said something about *what happened*, then some scribbles she couldn't make out, then: *a mistake. I will* … then a bit she couldn't read … *Bunny so we can make a life together. I'm sorry if* … another scribbled line, then: *I love you and will always remember this night. Paudie.*

Megan squinted at the note. Could it be true? Did he think what had happened between them was… a mistake? She tried to read it again. No, it was impossible. His handwriting, normally hard enough to read, was, in this hastily scribbled state, no more than hieroglyphics. *It can't be,* she thought. *It must mean he loves me… Oh, why didn't I find this note that morning? But why didn't he answer my messages? Why hasn't he been in touch?*

The cleaning forgotten, Megan decided to go and find Paudie and finally get an answer. She got up and grabbed her jacket. After locking the back door, she went around the corner of the house and walked straight into him.

They looked at each other in shock.

"Paudie," Megan said.

There was a flash of pain in his eyes. "Hello. I've come to get my sheep. They're going up the mountains." His voice had a cold edge she had never heard before.

"Yes, of course." Megan looked at his strong hands and remembered their gentle touch on her bare skin. He was standing so close she could smell his own particular scent of soap and grass. She took a step back, noticing the chest hairs in the open neck of his shirt, his strong chin with faint stubble and finally looked into his bright blue eyes.

"If that's all right with you," he added in this new cold voice.

She felt tears well up and swallowed, trying desperately to appear cool and unperturbed. "That's okay," she heard herself say. "You go ahead."

His eyes softer, he stepped closer. Put his finger under her chin and tilted her face. "Megan? What happened? Why didn't you answer my note?"

Confused, she stared at him. "I didn't find it until just now. But I did leave a message on your voicemail that morning. And then, when I got no reply, sent you a text."

He stared at her blankly. "I got no such message. I checked my phone constantly. I needed to know how you felt after reading that note."

Anger surged in Megan's chest and stopped the tears. "Never mind the message. How the fuck, do you think I felt?" she spat. "You just left me there, after we... after... you know. Then I tried to phone you but only got your voicemail. I left a message, then a text. You didn't reply, so I thought you—" She tried to pull herself together. "I only found that note today, you know. Just now. It had blown in under the sofa. But that's beside the point. What was in the message was quite clear to me. You said it was a mistake. You said that you and Bunny—"

His eyes widened. "What are you talking about? That's not at all what I said in my note. Don't you know how to read?"

"I read very well, thank you," she said stiffly. "But perhaps you could learn how to write? Of course I couldn't make out all that was in the note. Your handwriting's crap. But I got the most important bits."

He moved closer again and grabbed her shoulders. Dark with anger, his eyes bored into hers. "What the fuck are you saying? I wrote that I left you sleeping and would be back later. That our... the... you know, what we did was truly beautiful. That my relationship with Bunny was a mistake. That I was going to break up with her so we could make a life together, you and I. And finally, that I love you. What part of that didn't you get?"

Megan gasped. His fingers dug into her arms, his eyes full of pain and hurt. "I... she started. "What? I can't ... Please let me go, and I'll tell you."

He let her go so fast she nearly fell. Megan stumbled but regained her balance. She tried to speak but couldn't get the words out. "I..." she started. " Oh God, Paudie." She burst into tears. "The note blew off the table. The window was open and a sudden gust of wind blew everything around." She gulped, fighting for breath. "I didn't see it until just now, a moment ago. Those words were all I was able to read. The ones about 'a mistake' and Bunny and how you wanted to make a life together with her. I thought..." she ended feebly.

He frowned. "And those three words at the end? What did you think that was all about?"

Megan sniffed and wiped her nose with her sleeve. "Those words were a great help. I thought that maybe you do—did—love me but felt I wasn't right for you and that Bunny would be a much better companion." She stopped for breath and looked at Paudie for help, for reassurance or at least something to blow her nose in. "Have you a hanky?"

Paudie dug in his pocket and handed her a clean but crumpled handkerchief. "Here. Blow your nose."

She took it. "It's not ironed. Bunny on strike?"

"She's gone. I broke up with her that night. She left the next day."

"Oh." She stared at him. "She left that morning? Were you there when she left?"

"No. I went out to check the cattle. When I came back, she was gone."

Something occurred to Megan. "What time was that? I mean, what time did you go out?"

He looked confused. "Why? Around nine o'clock or something."

"And then Bunny was on her own, packing?"

"Yes." He frowned. "Why are you asking these questions?"

"Never mind. Just listen. I suppose you didn't have your phone with you when you were checking the cattle?"

Paudie put his hand to his forehead. "Shit! No, I didn't. What time did you call me?"

"Around half past nine."

They stared at each other.

"I suppose you had a row?" Megan said.

"Yes. It was quite bitter. She was very upset. In fact, she nearly spat in my face when I mentioned you."

Megan wiped her nose. "Of course. Well, there's your answer. She must have deleted my messages."

Paudie nodded. "Must have. The sneaky bitch."

"Well, the woman scorned and all that. Must say I don't blame her." Megan stopped. "But that doesn't excuse you not calling me again. Or trying to find out why I hadn't called you."

"Why didn't *you* call me again?" he demanded. "Shit, Megan, did you really think I'd use you for a quick screw and then just run off. What do you take me for, huh?"

Megan's shoulders slumped. "I didn't know," she whispered. "I was scared. I thought…" She couldn't go on, but stood there, willing him to understand, to realise that because of what she had been through in the not so distant past had made her distrustful of men. "I couldn't believe you loved me."

He didn't seem to have heard. His eyes were devoid of expression as he digested all she had said.

"Paudie?" Megan whispered. "Say something. Please."

He shook his head. "Don't know what to say. I can see how the note might have been difficult to decipher. But…" He paused. "You didn't trust me. You thought I'd give you up for Bunny because she was more suitable? Or that I didn't have the guts to break up with her? Why the fuck didn't you come and ask me?"

Megan shrugged and sniffled. "But I did. I left those messages on your phone. Then when there was no reply, I thought—" She stopped. "Actually, I was on my way to see you right now." She looked at him accusingly. "But why didn't you ask *me* what was going on? Why didn't you try a little harder?"

"I don't play games. I say what I say, and if that's not good enough, too bad."

"Too bloody proud, that's your problem," Megan snapped. "Well, in that case, I could return the favour and say you didn't trust me either."

"I suppose you're right." He stopped. "Which means we shouldn't go any further. If we don't trust each other, we won't get on. Ever."

"Probably." The urge to throw her arms around him and beg for forgiveness was nearly unbearable. She took a step back. "I'm going for a walk on the beach."

"I'll load up the sheep, then."

"Good."

"Right."

Silence. Megan sniffled. "Is that it?"

"Yeah," he growled. He turned his back to her and walked back to the jeep and trailer.

Megan wanted to run after him. She wanted to touch his arm to ask, plead, beg, but the stiffness in his gait and his rigid shoulders told her there was no point. She blew her nose in Paudie's hankie and half ran up the path to the dunes and the beach.

She walked for over an hour, the sea roaring in her ears, the wind whipping her hair into thick, hard strands. The wild weather felt like a punishment she knew she deserved but it didn't cure her desperate need to be with Paudie. *He must feel the same. I'll give him a little time, and then he'll soften. Maybe he's waiting for me,* she thought and ran back to the house. But when she got there, he was gone.

* * *

Hours passed. Days. Nights.

Time goes so slowly when you're in pain, Megan thought, trying to busy herself as best she could. The trip to Paris was a great help, and she threw herself into setting up her website, making it as professional and marketable as she could. Her wardrobe needed a good going over, and she sorted out all her clothes, picking the best items for a week in Paris. She had wisely kept the best designer outfits from her past life as a stylist and now found at least three outfits she could combine into a clean, classy look. She had her hair cut and even splurged on a day at a spa in Killarney for a top-to-toe overhaul. Suitably buffed, coiffed and dressed, she set off for Shannon airport early one morning to leave for Paris.

The departure hall was busy, and there was already a long queue for the Paris flight. Megan joined the back of the queue and put down her suitcase. She was checking her handbag for her passport and ticket, when someone touched her arm.

She looked up and blinked. "Paudie?"

"Yes, it's me." Dressed in a suede jacket and beige chinos, his hair brushed, he looked unusually polished and glamorous. His eyes on her were tender and a little shy. "You look beautiful."

"Thank you. What are you doing here?"

He smiled. "Came to say goodbye and bon voyage."

"Oh? Why? I thought you'd never want to speak to me again."

He looked at her for a while without replying. "Oh, I didn't. For a long time. But then I came to miss my best friend. There was nobody to needle me or ask awkward questions. No one to share my cold pizza. My sock drawer's a mess. My life was too quiet and easy."

"And boring?" Megan shuffled forward as the queue moved.

"Yes." He took her arm and leaned against her. "Can we move away from here?" he whispered in her ear. "Too many people listening."

"But I have to check in. I'm going to Paris."

He looked at the sign over the check-in desk. "So I gather. But then, I can read."

She stifled a laugh. "How did you know I was here?"

"Diana. She told me early this morning when I helped her move the horses. I said I didn't know where you were and that I needed to talk to you. So she took one look at my miserable face and said 'go after her, you fool'. So I did. Took me a while to clean up." He looked at Megan sheepishly. "But here I am. A big fool."

"Yes. And your hair is sticking up at the back."

He patted it down. "Didn't have time to style it."

"It looks good. *You* look good. Oh, I'm nearly there." Megan took out her passport. "Not much time. But you can walk me to the security gate."

"Thank you, Your Highness. That's a great honour."

Megan giggled. She checked in her suitcase and gathered up her boarding pass. "We only have a few minutes. My flight will be boarding soon."

"I know."

They walked together across the vast departures hall and came to a stop in front of the escalator. Paudie put his hands on Megan's shoulders and looked deep into her eyes. He took a deep breath. "I love you."

She felt tears well up. "Oh, Paudie. And I love you. I really do."

"No need to say more then, is there?"

"No. And I'll be back in a week."

"Good. You go to Paris, girl, and have a good time. That's an order."

"Yes, sir." Megan laughed between tears and put her arms around his waist. "I have to go," she whispered into his neck.

"I know. Just one more thing. Give me your hand."

"Why?" she lifted her right hand.

"Because." He took the Claddagh ring, pulled it off her finger and turned it around, placing it on the third finger of her left hand. "See? Now the point of the crown is toward your finger. You know what that means?"

She nodded. "I do." She looked up at him. "I'll wear it like this from now on."

"Yes," he said. "You will. Always."

THE END

ABOUT THE AUTHOR:

Susanne O'Leary was born in Sweden and lives in Ireland (married to an Irishman). She started her writing career by writing non-fiction and wrote two books about health and fitness (She is also a trained fitness teacher). While writing these books, she discovered how much she loved the actual writing process. Her then editor gave her the idea to write a fun novel based on her experiences as a diplomat's wife. This became her debut novel, 'Diplomatic Incidents' (the e-book version is called 'Duty Free'), published in 2001. She wrote three further novels, 'European Affairs' (now as an e-book with the title 'Villa Caramel'), 'Fresh Powder' (2006) and 'Finding Margo' (2007). The latter two were published by New Island Books in Dublin.

In 2010, when the publishing industry started to decline, Susanne broke away from both publisher and agent and e-published her backlist, along with two novels that were with her agent for submission. Since then she has written and e-published five further novels and, as a result, now has eleven books out there in the e-book market worldwide. Susanne writes mainly in the women's fiction genre, some chick-lit, some contemporary romance, with two historical novels and two detective stories thrown into the mix. She enjoyed writing those but her first love is romantic fiction with a lot of humour and heart. Susanne's bestselling romantic comedy, Fresh Powder was translated to German last year and, with the title 'Frischer Schnee', is selling well on Amazon.de.

Susanne is currently working on a sequel to Hot Property, which will be published at the end of 2013.

Susanne loves to hear from her readers. You can contact her through her website: http://www.susanne-oleary.com

Susanne's blog: http://susannefromsweden.wordpress.com/

Amazon author page:
http://www.amazon.com/Susanne-OLeary/e/B001JOXAJO